THE CORNER HOUSE GIRLS' ODD FIND

BY

GRACE BROOKS HILL

THE CORNER HOUSE GIRLS ODD FIND

CHAPTER I—A FIND IN THE GARRET

The fireboard before the great chimney-place in the spacious dining room of the old Corner House in Milton had been removed by Uncle Rufus, and in the dusk of the winter's afternoon the black pit of it yawned, ogre-like, upon the festive room.

The shadows were black under the big tree, the tip of which touched the very high ceiling and which had just been set up in the far corner and not yet festooned. The girls were all busy bringing tinsel and glittering balls and cheery red bells and strings of pink and white popcorn, while yards and yards of evergreen "rope," with which to trim the room itself, were heaped in a corner.

It was the day but one before Christmas, and without the gaslight—or even the usual gas-log fire on the hearth—the dining room was gloomy even at mid-afternoon. Whenever Dot Kenway passed the black opening under the high and ornate mantel, she shuddered.

It was a creepy, delicious shudder that the smallest Corner House girl experienced, for she said to Tess, her confidant and the next oldest of the four sisters:

"Of course, I know it's the only way Santa Claus ever comes. But—but I should think he'd be afraid of—of rats or things. I don't see why he can't come in at the door; it'd be more respecterful."

"I s'pose you mean respectable," sighed Tess. "But where would he hitch his reindeer? You know he has to tie them to the chimney on the roof."

"Why does he?" demanded the inquisitive Dot. "There's a perfectly good hitching post by our side gate on Willow Street."

"Who ever heard of such a thing!" exclaimed Tess, with exasperation. "Do you s'pose Santa Claus would come to the side door and knock like the old clo's man? You are the most ridiculous child, Dot Kenway," concluded Tess, with her most grown-up air.

"Say," said the quite unabashed Dot, reflectively, "do you know what Sammy Pinkney says?"

"Nothing very good, I am sure," rejoined her sister, tartly, for just at this time Sammy Pinkney, almost their next-door neighbor, was very much in Tess Kenway's bad books. "What can you expect of a boy who wants to be a pirate?"

"Well," Dot proclaimed, "Sammy says he doesn't believe there is such a person as Santa Claus."

"Oh!" gasped Tess, startled by this heresy. Then, after reflection, she added: "Well, when you come to think of it, I don't suppose there is any Santa for Sammy Pinkney."

"Oh, Tess!" almost groaned the smaller girl.

"No, I don't," repeated Tess, with greater confidence. "Ruthie says if we don't 'really and truly' believe in Santa, there isn't any—for us! And he only comes to good children, anyway. How could you expect Sammy Pinkney to have a Santa Claus?"

"He says," said Dot, eagerly, "that they are only make believe. Why, there is one in Blachstein & Mapes', where Ruth trades; and another in Millikin's; and there's the Salvation Army Santa Clauses on the streets—"

"Pooh!" exclaimed Tess, tossing her head. "They are only representations of Santa Claus. They're men dressed up. Why! little boys have Santa Claus suits to play in, just as they have Indian suits and cowboy suits."

"But—but is there really and truly a Santa Claus?" questioned Dot, in an awed tone. "And does he keep a book with your name in it? And if you don't get too many black marks through the year do you get presents? And if you do behave too badly will he leave a whip, or something nasty, in your stocking? Say, Tess, do you s'pose 'tis so?"

That was a stiff one—even for Tess Kenway's abounding faith. She was silent for a moment.

"Say! do you?" repeated the smallest Corner House girl.

"I tell you, Dot," Tess said, finally, "I want to believe it. I just do. It's like fairies and elfs. We want to believe in them, don't we? It's just like your Alice-doll being alive."

"Well!" exclaimed Dot, stoutly, "she's just as good as alive!"

"Of course she is, Dottie," said Tess, eagerly. "And so's Santa Claus. And—and when we stop believing in him, we won't have near so much fun at Christmas!"

Just then Agnes came in from the kitchen with a heaping pan of warm popcorn.

"Here, you kiddies," she cried, "run and get your needles and thread. We haven't near enough popcorn strung. I believe Neale O'Neil ate more than he strung last night, I never did see such a hungry boy!"

"Mrs. MacCall say it's 'cause he's growning," said Dot, solemnly.

"He, he!" chuckled Agnes. "He should be 'groaning' after all he gobbled down last night. And I burned my finger and roasted my face, popping it."

She set down the dish of flaky white puff-balls on a stool, so it would be handy for the little girls. Both brought their sewing boxes and squatted down on the floor in the light from a long window. Tess was soon busily threading the popcorn.

"What's the matter with you, Dot Kenway?" she demanded, as the smallest Corner House girl seemed still to be fussing with her thread and needle, her face puckered up and a frown on her small brow. "You're the slowest thing!"

"I—I believe this needle's asleep, Tess," wailed Dot, finally.

"Asleep?" gasped the other. "What nonsense!"

"Yes, 'tis—so now!" ejaculated Dot. "Anyway, I can't get its eye open."

A low laugh sounded behind them, and a tall girl swooped down on the floor and put her arms around the smallest Corner House girl.

"Let sister do it for you, honeybee," said the newcomer. "Won't the eye open? Well! we'll make it—there!"

This was Ruth, the oldest of the four Kenway sisters. She was dark, not particularly pretty, but, as Tess often said, awfully good! Ruth had a smile that illuminated her rather plain face and won her friends everywhere. Moreover, she had a beautiful, low, sweet voice—a "mother voice," Agnes said.

Ruth had been mothering her three younger sisters for a long time now—ever since their real mother had died, leaving Agnes and Tess and Dot, to say nothing of Aunt Sarah Maltby, in the older girl's care. And faithfully had Ruth Kenway performed her duty.

Agnes was the pretty sister (although Tess, with all her gravity, promised to equal the fly-away in time) for she had beautiful light hair, a rosy complexion, and large blue eyes, of an expression most innocent but in the depths of which lurked the Imps of Mischief.

Little Dot was dark, like Ruth; only she was most lovely—her hair wavy and silky, her little limbs round, her eyes bright, and her lips as red as an ox-heart cherry!

The little girls went on stringing the popcorn, and Ruth and Agnes began to trim the tree, commencing at the very top. Nestling among the pointed branches of the fir was a winged cupid, with bow and arrow.

"That's so much better than a bell. Everybody has bells," said Agnes, from the step-ladder, as she viewed the cupid with satisfaction.

"It's an awfully cunning little fat, white baby," agreed Dot, from the floor. "But I should be afraid, if I were his mother, to let him play with bows-an'-arrows. Maybe he'll prick himself."

"We'll speak to Venus about that," chuckled Agnes. "Don't believe anybody ever mentioned it to her."

"'Venus'?" repeated Dot, gravely. "Why, that's the name of the lady that lives next to Uncle Rufus' Petunia. She couldn't be that little baby's mother for she's—oh!—awful black!"

"Aggie was speaking of another Venus, Dot," laughed Ruth. "Fasten those little candle-holders securely, Aggie."

"Sure!" agreed the second, and slangy, sister.

"I really wish we could light the whole room with candles, and not have the gas at all," Ruth said. "It would be much nicer. Don't you think so?"

"It would be scrumptious!" Aggie cried. "And you've got such a lot of those nice, fat, bayberry candles. Let's do it!"

"But there are not enough candlesticks."

"You can get 'em at the five-and-ten-cent store," proposed Tess, who favored that busy emporium, "because you can get such a lot for your money!"

"Goosey!" exclaimed Agnes. "We don't want cheap ones. How would they look beside those lovely old silver ones of Uncle Peter Stower's?" and she turned to look at the great candelabra on the highboy.

Just then the door from the butler's pantry opened slowly and a grizzled, kinky head, with a shiny, brown, bald spot on top, was thrust into the room.

"I say, missie!" drawled the voice belonging to the ancient head, "is yo' done seen anyt'ing ob dat denim bag I has fo' de soiled napkins? Pechunia, she done comin' fo' de wash, an' I got t' collect togeddah all I kin fin' dis week. Dat fool brack woman," Uncle Rufus added with disgust, "won't do but dis one wash twill happen New Years—naw'm! She jes' got t' cel'brate, she say. Ma' soul! what's a po', miserble nigger woman got t' cel'brate fo' Ah asks ye?"

"Why, Uncle Rufus!" cried Agnes. "Christmas is a birthday that everybody ought to celebrate. And I'm sure Petunia has many things to make her happy."

"Just look at all her children!" put in Tess.

"Alfredia, and Jackson Montgomery Simms, and little Burne-Jones Whistler and Louise Annette," Dot began to intone, naming the roll of Petunia Blossom's piccaninnies.

"Don't! Stop!" begged Agnes, with her hands over her ears and sitting down on the top step of the ladder.

"Ma soul!" chuckled Uncle Rufus, "if chillens come lak' Chris'mus presents, all de rich w'ite folks would hab 'em an' de po' nigger folks would be habbin' wot de paper calls 'race sooincide'—sho' would!"

"I haven't seen the laundry bag, Unc' Rufus," said Ruth, deep in thought.

Here Dot spoke up. "I 'spect I know where it is, Unc' Rufus," she said.

"Wal! I 'spected some ob yo' chillen done had it."

"You know," said Dot, seriously, "my Alice-doll is real weakly. The doctors don't give me much 'couragement about her. Her lungs are weak—they have been, you know, ever since that awful Trouble girl buried her with the dried apples."

"Dat Lillie Treble. Ah 'members hit—sho!" chuckled Uncle Rufus, the Corner House girls' chief factotum, who was a tall, thin, brown old negro, round shouldered with age, but "spry and pert," as he said himself.

"And the doctors," went on Dot, waxing serious, and her imagination "working over time," as Neale O'Neil would have said, "say it's best for folks with weak lungs to sleep out of doors. So Neale's built her a sleeping porch outside one of the windows in our bedroom—Tess' and mine—and—and I used your napkin bag, Unc' Rufus, for a sleeping-bag for my Alice-doll! I couldn't find anything else that fitted her," confessed the smallest Corner House girl.

"Well! of all the children!" cried Agnes, having taken her hands down from her ears to hear this.

"You shouldn't have taken the bag without permission," Ruth gravely told Dot.

But Uncle Rufus chuckled over it to a great extent. "Nebber did see de beat of dese young-uns!" he gasped finally. "If yo' Uncle Peter was alive he sartain sho' would ha' laffed hisself up out'n hes sick-bed. Ma soul an' body! W'y didn't he know enough t' hab yo'uns yere in de ol' Corner House w'ile he was alive, 'stid o' waitin' till he was daid t' gib it t' yo'?"

He would have gone out chuckling, only Ruth called after him: "Unc' Rufus! Do you know if there are any more candlesticks around the house? Nice, heavy ones, I mean—good enough to put in the dining room here, and for company to see."

"Candlesticks, missie? I 'spect dere is," said the old negro man.

"Do you know where?" Ruth asked quickly.

"Bress yo', honey! I 'speck dey is up in de attic," he said. "I don' jes' know whar—"

"Oh, I know! I know!" cried Agnes, suddenly. "Over in that corner of the garret that we never cleaned, Ruth."

"Did we fail to clear up any part of the garret?" asked the older girl, doubtfully.

"The place Tommy Rooney hid in when he was the attic goat," Dot said solemnly.

"Ghost!" admonished Tess. "I do wish you'd get your words right, Dot Kenway."

"I remember seeing some old brass candlesticks there," Agnes went on to explain to Ruth. "They can be polished, I should think. They're all green now."

"Of course," said Ruth, cheerfully. "Let's go and look for them."

"Oh, I want to go!" cried Dot, at once.

"May we all go, sister?" asked Tess.

"Of course you may come, kiddies," said Agnes, hopping down from her perch.

They all trooped up the three flights of stairs to the huge garret, Dot leaving her "sleeping" needle sticking in a puff-ball of popcorn.

The front hall of the old Corner House, as Milton folk called the Stower homestead on the corner of Willow Street, opposite the Parade Ground, was two stories high.

Broad stairs, dividing when half way up into two separate flights, rose out of the middle of the reception hall, lined with its old-fashioned, walnut, haircloth furniture. A gallery ran all around the stair-well, off which opened the guest chambers of the house. Only one of these was in use. Aunt Sarah Maltby had it. Aunt Sarah was determined to have the best there was of everything.

The girls slept in rooms in one of the two ells, on this second floor. Above, in the third story of the same ell, slept Mrs. MacCall, their good Scotch housekeeper, and Linda, the Finnish girl. Uncle Rufus was stowed away in the other ell, in a little room he had occupied for almost twenty-six years. Uncle Rufus had been Uncle Peter Stower's only retainer for many, many years before the Kenway girls came to live at the old Corner House.

Up another flight of stairs, the girls trooped to the garret, that extended the entire length and breadth of the main portion of the house. This was their playroom on rainy days, and a storeroom of wonderful things. The Kenways had never entirely exhausted the wonders of this place.

Agnes led the way to the far corner, lamp in hand. There some Revolutionary uniforms hung from the low rafters. On a broken-legged chest of drawers, held up by a brick in place of the missing leg, stood a row of heavy brass candlesticks.

"And see here!" cried Agnes, snatching up a faded, fat, plush-covered volume, moth-eaten and shabby, from which Ruth had just removed two of the candlesticks. "What can this be? The family album, I declare!"

She flirted several of the leaves. Others stuck together. There seemed to be some kind of illustrations, or pictures, between the pages.

"Throw that dusty old thing down, Aggie," said Ruth, "and help me carry these heavy candlesticks. They are just the things."

"I'll help carry them," agreed her sister. "Here, Dottums. You can just about lug this old book. I want to look at it. I shouldn't wonder if it held daguerreotypes and silhouettes of all the Stowers since Adam."

"What are da—da-gert-o-tops and—and silly-hats, Aggie?" demanded Dot, toiling along at the end of the procession with the big book, as the four girls started down stairs again. "Are—are they those awful animals Ruth was reading about that used to in—infest the earth so long ago?"

"Oh, mercy me!" gasped Agnes, laughing. "Pterodactyls and the giant sloth! See what it means to tell these kids about the Paleozoic age and 'sich,' Ruthie! Yes, child. Maybe you'll find pictures in that old book of those 'critters,' as Mrs. Mac calls them."

Dot sat right down on the upper flight and spread the book out upon her small lap. She had heard just enough about the creatures of the ancient world to be vitally curious.

But there were no pictures of animals. Dot hurriedly turned the pages. In the back were engravings on green paper, stuck into the old book. The green slips of paper had pictures on them, but nothing that interested Dot.

"Pooh!" she thought to herself, did the smallest Corner House girl, "old money—that's all it is. Just like the money Mr. Howbridge gives Ruth every month to pay bills with. I s'pose it's money that's no good any more."

She shut the book, disappointed, and clattered down stairs after her sisters. Nobody else had time to look at the family album just then. Agnes tossed her "find" into a corner until some more convenient occasion for looking at it. She and Ruth got the metal cleaning paste and rags and a chamois, and began to polish the candlesticks. The smaller girls returned to the stringing of popcorn.

Suddenly they all stopped work. With upraised hands and astonished looks, the four listened for a repetition of the sound that had startled them.

It came again, immediately. It was in the chimney. There was a muffled shout, then a scratching and a scraping, coming rapidly down the brick-and-mortar tunnel.

"Oh! Oh! OH!" squealed Dot, in crescendo. "Santa Claus has come ahead of time!"

"If that's Santa Claus," declared Agnes, jumping up to run to the open fireplace, "he's missed his footing and is falling down the chimney!"

CHAPTER II—"A PERFECTLY SAVAGE SANTA CLAUS"

Mrs. MacCall put her head into the dining room just as the girls rushed to the chimney-place to see what the noise within it meant. The housekeeper asked:

"Did you girls see that little imp, Sam Pinkney? Linda says he came through the kitchen a while ago, and when he heard you had gone to the garret he went up the back stairs to find you."

"Sammy Pinkney!" chorused the two smallest Corner House girls.

"Well! it isn't Santa then," added Dot, with immense relief.

"It's that imp, sure enough!" cried Agnes.

And just then a sooty bundle bounced down upon the hearth, to the unbounded amusement, if not amazement, of the Kenway sisters and Mrs. MacCall.

Ever since the Kenway girls had come to Milton and the old Corner House, Sammy Pinkney had been an abundant source of exasperation, amusement, and wonder to them all—especially to Tess and Dot.

Their coming to the Corner House, and all its attendant adventure and mystery, is chronicled in the first book of the series, entitled "The Corner House Girls." The Kenways and Aunt Sarah Maltby had been very poor in the city where they had lived in a cheap tenement. All they had for support was a small pension. Aunt Sarah proclaimed always that when Peter Stower, of Milton, who was her half brother, died, "they would all be rich enough." But that was only "talk," so Ruth thought.

One day, however, Mr. Howbridge, a lawyer, came to see the orphans. He had been Uncle Peter's man of business and was now administrator of the estate, Uncle Peter having died suddenly.

The lawyer told Ruth that he knew Uncle Peter had left a will making the Kenway girls his heirs-at-law—and leaving a very small legacy indeed to Aunt Sarah. But Uncle Peter was queer, and at the last had hidden the will. The lawyer said the Kenways must come and occupy the old Corner House in Milton until the will was found.

Aunt Sarah came with them of course. She considered herself very badly used, and acted as though she thought the best of everything in their new station in life should be hers. The Court made Mr. Howbridge the girls' guardian, and the four sisters lived a rather precarious existence at the old Corner House for the first few months, for they were not at all sure that they were in their rightful place.

Indeed, when "the lady from Ypsilanti" with her little girl came along, and the lady claimed that she and Lillie were Uncle Peter's rightful heirs, Ruth took them in and treated them kindly in the absence of Mr. Howbridge, fearing that the strangers might have a better claim upon the estate than themselves.

Finally this Mrs. Treble (whom Agnes called "Mrs. Trouble," and her little girl, "Double Trouble") aroused Aunt Sarah's antagonism. To get them out of the house the queer old woman showed Ruth where Uncle Peter Stower had been wont to hide his private papers.

In this secret hiding place was the lost will. It established the rights of the Corner House girls to the estate and settled them firmly in the Stower homestead.

In the second volume of the series, "The Corner House Girls at School," the girls extended the field of their acquaintance, entered the local schools, and became the friends, and finally the confidants, of Neale O'Neil, the boy who had run away away from Twomley & Sorber's Herculean Circus and Menagerie, to get an education and "be like other boys."

Neale was not the only person the Corner House girls befriended in this and the third book: "The Corner House Girls Under Canvas." The latter story relates their adventures at Pleasant Cove, where they went for their vacation the second summer of their sojourn in the old Corner House, and during which time they were the means of reuniting Rosa Wildwood, one of Ruth's schoolmates, to her sister, June, who had been living with a tribe of Gypsies.

Back again in the fall, and at school, Tess and Dot chance to meet Mrs. Eland, matron of the Women's and Children's Hospital, an institution doing excellent work in Milton, but not much appreciated by the townspeople at large. Tess quite falls in love with Mrs. Eland and is horrified to learn that the lonely woman is likely to lose her position, and the hospital to be closed, because of lack of funds.

Without any real idea of what she is accomplishing, Tess Kenway goes about talking to anybody and everybody of the hospital's need. She completely stirs up the town regarding the institution.

The schools take the matter up and the Board of Education approves a plan for the pupils to give a play for the benefit of the Women's and Children's Hospital. Each member of the Corner House quartette had a part in the play, and the performances of The Carnation Countess had but just been given during the fore part of this very Christmas week.

The narrative of these recent occurrences may be found in the fourth volume of the series, the story immediately preceding this one, called "The Corner House Girls in a Play." Three thousand dollars was raised for the hospital, and Mrs. Eland—Tess' "little gray lady"—is assured of the continuation of her situation as matron.

This fact is particularly happy at this time, for Mrs. Eland's sister, Miss Pepperill, Tess' school teacher, is ill, and Mrs. Eland is nursing her back to health. One reason for the decorating of the Corner House dining room is that the reunited sisters, Mrs. Eland and Miss Pepperill, have been invited to eat their Christmas dinner with the Corner House girls.

All this while the sooty bundle was lying on the brick hearth at the feet of the startled Corner House girls. As it squirmed, and the sooty dust arose from it, they saw that it was certainly alive.

It wore a long cloak and a hood, now of a sooty red, and trimmed with what was once white cotton-wool "fur." Leggings of the same material and trimming covered a pair of stout nether limbs; and upon these legs the little figure finally scrambled, revealing at last to the Kenway sisters and to Mrs. MacCall a face as black as any negro's.

"For pity's sake!" exclaimed the housekeeper. "What d' you call that, anyway?"

"It—it's Sammy," said Tess, boldly.

"If it is Santa Claus," said Ruth, smiling, "it is one that is not grown."

"It's a perfectly savage one," chuckled Agnes. "This must be a young Santa Claus in his wild and untamed state."

"He is unfamiliar with the best methods of descending folks' chimneys, that is sure," Ruth pursued. "I don't think this Santa Claus has learned his trade yet."

"And—and how black he is!" murmured Dot. "Are—are all Santa Clauses so black?"

"Aw, you girls make me sick!" growled the much abashed Santa Claus.

"I declare—he talks our language!" cried Agnes.

"Why, of course," said Tess, the literal. "He's in my class at school, you know."

"You think you are all so smart!" sneered Sammy Pinkney, and that sneer was something awful to behold. Dot fairly shuddered.

"You wait!" snarled Sammy. "When I run away and get to be a pirate, I'll—I'll—I'll—"

Sammy's emotion choked him for the moment. Mrs. MacCall sniffed; Ruth began to speak soothingly; Agnes giggled; Tess looked her disapproval of the savage young Santa Claus; while Dot, who had caught up the Alice-doll and squeezed her protectingly to her breast, gasped:

"Oh! Oh! Isn't he dreadful?"

Sammy's sharp ear evidently caught the smallest Corner House girl's whisper, for he rolled an approving eye in Dot's direction, and finally finished his fearsome peroration with true piratical savagery:

"I'll come back and I'll make every one of you walk the plank!"

"What ever that may mean," murmured Agnes, quite weak from laughter. But as Sammy Pinkney started for the door she cried: "Oh, Sammy!"

"Well? What's the matter?" growled the savage young Santa Claus.

"Tell us—do! How did you get in the chimney?" asked Agnes.

"The skylight was open when I followed you girls upstairs, so I got up on the roof and crawled in at the top of the chimbley. It was all right coming down, too," said the young rascal, "till I got to the second story. There was irons in the chimbley for steps; but one was loose and fell out when I stepped on it. Then I—I slipped."

He stalked out. Dot said ruminatively: "We'd better have that step fixed before to-morrow night, hadn't we, Ruthie? Before Santa Claus comes, you know. He might fall and hurt himself."

"Very true, Dottums," declared Agnes, with a quickly serious face. "I'll speak to Uncle Rufus about it."

But Agnes must have forgotten, or else Uncle Rufus did not attend to the missing step in the chimney. At least, so Dot supposed when she awoke in the dark the very next morning and heard something going "thump-thumpity-thump" down the chimney again.

The smallest Corner House girl was not in the habit of waking up when it seemed still "the middle of the night," and her small head was quite confused. She really thought it must be Christmas morning and that good Kris Kringle has suffered a bad fall.

"Oh-ee! if he's brought Alice-doll her new carriage, it will be all smashed!" gasped Dot, and she slipped out of bed without disturbing Tess.

She shrugged on her little bathrobe and put her tiny feet into slippers. Somebody ought to go to see how bad a fall Santa Claus had—and see if all his presents were smashed. Dot really had forgotten that there was still another day before Christmas.

The little girl padded out of her room and along the hall to the front of the house. Nobody heard her as she descended the front stairs.

Dot came to the foot of the stairs, where a single dim gaslight flickered. She pushed open the dining room door.

As she did so, there sounded the faint clink, clink, clink of metal against metal. A spotlight flashed and roved around the room—touching ceiling and walls and floor in its travels. But it did not reveal her figure just inside the door.

She saw no good Kris Kringle standing on the hearth, with his bag of toys. Nothing but a broken brick lay there—probably loosened by Sammy Pinkney in his course down the chimney-well the previous afternoon.

There was a shadowy figure—she could not see its face—stooping over a cloth laid upon the floor; and upon that cloth was stacked much of the choice old silver which Uncle Rufus always packed away so carefully after using in the locked safe in the butler's pantry.

CHAPTER III—DOROTHY'S BURGLAR

Dot Kenway had heard about burglars. That is, she knew there were such people. Just why they went about "burgling," as she herself phrased it, the smallest Corner House girl did not understand.

But she thought, with a queer jumping at her heart, that she had found a "really truly" burglar now.

He was just putting their very best sugar-bowl on the top of the pile of other silver, and she expected to see him tie up the cloth by its four corners preparatory to taking it away.

Dot really did not know what she ought to do. Of course, she might have screamed for Ruth; but then, she knew that Ruthie would be awfully scared if she did.

Why, Tess, even, would be scared if she came across a burglar! Dot was quite sure of that; and she felt happy to know that she was really not so scared as she supposed she would have been.

The burglar did not seem any more fearful in appearance than the iceman, or the man who took out the ashes, or the man who came to sharpen the knives and had a key-bugle—

Oh! and maybe burglars carried something to announce their calling, like other tradesmen. The junkman had a string of bells on his wagon; the peanutman had a whistle on his roaster; the man who mended tinware and umbrellas beat a shiny new tin pan as he walked through Willow Street—

"Oh!" ejaculated the curious Dot, right out loud, "do you use a whistle, or a bell, or anything, in your business, please?"

My goodness! how that man jumped! Dot thought he would fall right over backward, and the round ray of the spotlight in his hand shot up to the ceiling and all about the room before it fell on Dot, standing over by the hall door.

"Well, I'll be jiggered!" gasped the man, in utter amazement. "Wha—what did you say, miss?"

He was not really a man, after all. Dot saw by his lean face that he was nothing more than a half grown boy. So every little bit of fear she had felt for the burglar departed. He could not really be a journeyman burglar—only an apprentice, just learning his trade. Dot became confidential at once, and came closer to him.

"I—I never met anybody in your business before," said the smallest Corner House girl. "If you please, do you only come into folks's houses at night?"

"Huh!" croaked the young man, hoarsely. "Seems ter me we're workin' both night an' day at this season. I never did see it so hard on a poor feller before."

"Oh, my!" exclaimed Dot. "Do you have busy seasons, and slack seasons, like the peddlers?"

"I should say we did, miss," agreed the other, still in a complaining tone.

"My! What makes this time of year a busy one?" demanded the inquisitive Dorothy.

"The frost, miss."

"The frost?" repeated the little girl, quite puzzled.

"Yes, miss. The frost catches folks napping, as ye may say."

Dot puzzled over that for a moment, too. Did folks sleep harder when it was frosty and dark out-of-doors, than in summer? The young man stood and watched her. It must be rather embarrassing to be interrupted in the midst of a burglary.

"Don't—don't mind me," said Dot, politely. "Don't let me stop your work."

"No, miss. I'm a-waiting for my boss," said the other.

There! Dot had known he must be only an apprentice burglar—he was so young.

"Then—then there's more of you?" she asked.

"More of me? No, ma'am," said the amazed young man. "You see all there is of me. I never was very husky—no, ma'am."

He seemed to be a very diffident burglar. He quite puzzled Dot.

"Don't—don't you ever get afraid in your business?" she asked. "I should think you would."

"Yep. I'm some afraid when I wipe a joint," admitted the young man. "Ye see, I ain't used to the hot lead, yet."

Dot thought over that answer a good while. Of course, she could not be expected to understand the professional talk of burglars—never having associated with that gentry. What "wiping a joint" meant she could not imagine; and what burglars did with hot lead was quite as puzzling.

"I—I suppose your boss is a journeyman burglar?" queried the little girl, at last.

"Wha-at!" gasped the young man. Then he grinned hugely. "That's what some of his customers calls him, miss," he agreed.

"Don't—don't you think there is some danger in your staying here alone?" asked Dot. "Suppose Uncle Rufus should come down stairs and catch you?"

"Hullo! who's Uncle Rufus?" asked the young man.

"Why—why, he's Uncle Rufus. He works for us—"

"Oh! he's the colored man?"

"Yes, sir."

"Why, he is down," said the young man, coolly. "He let us in. We had to come early, 'cause we've got so much work to do, and we didn't get through at Pinkney's till nine o'clock last night."

"At Pinkney's?" cried Dot, as the young man yawned. "Did—did you burgle Sammy's house, too?"

"What d'ye mean—'burgle'?" asked the young man, biting off the yawn and staring again at Dot.

"I beg your pardon," said Dot, gently. "But—but what do you call it?"

Just then the door of the butler's pantry opened and Uncle Rufus looked in.

"Dat oddah plumber done come, young man," he said. "Dis ain't no time in de mawnin'—'fo' six o'clock—t' come t' folks's houses nohow t' mend a busted watah-pipe—nossir! Yuh got all ob dem silber pieces out ob de safe?"

"They're all out, Uncle," said the young man.

"Whuffo' dey run dat pipe t'rough de silber closet, I dunno," complained the old darkey. "I use t' tell Mistah Peter Stowah dat it was one piece of plain foolishness. What if de bat'room is ober dis closet—"

He disappeared, his voice trailing off into silence, and the young man followed him. Dot was left breathless and rather abashed. Then the young man was not a burglar after all; he was only a plumber!

She crept back to bed, and said nothing to anybody about her early morning visit to the lower floor. But the young man told Uncle Rufus, and Uncle Rufus, chuckling hugely, told Mrs. MacCall.

"I'd like to know, for goodness' sake, what you would have done if it had been a really truly burglar, Dot Kenway?" Agnes demanded, when the story was repeated at the breakfast table.

"I'd have given him my silver knife and fork and mug, and asked him to go away without waking up Ruthie," declared the smallest Corner House girl, having thought it all out by that time.

"I believe you would—you blessed child!" cried Ruth, jumping up to kiss her.

"But suppose it had been Santa Claus?" Tess murmured, "and you had disturbed him filling our stockings?"

"Pooh!" said Dot. "If he'd felled down the chimbley like that brick, he wouldn't have been filling stockings."

CHAPTER IV—THE FAMILY ALBUM—AND OTHER THINGS

The day before Christmas was the busiest day of all. The dressing of the tree must be finished and the trimming and festooning of the big dining room completed. Neale O'Neil came over early to help the Corner House girls. He was a slim, rosy-cheeked, flaxen-haired boy, as agile as a monkey, and almost always smiling.

Ruth and Agnes would not hear to his helping trim the tree; but it was Neale's agility that made it possible for the rope of green to be festooned from the heavy ceiling cornices. Uncle Rufus was much too stiff with rheumatism for such work.

"Well! boys are some good, you must admit," Agnes said to Ruth, for the oldest Corner House girl was inclined to be a carping critic of the "mere male."

"All right. If he's so awfully useful, just let him clear up all this mess on the carpet, and then dust the rugs. Mercy, Agnes!" exclaimed Ruth, "what a lot of this green stuff there is all over the floor."

"Yes, I know," admitted Agnes.

"And there is other rubbish, too. Look at this old book you brought down from the attic and flung in the corner."

Ruth picked it up. It was heavy, and she carried it over to the broad window-seat on which she sat to open the "family album," as Agnes had called it.

The latter and Neale, having brought in basket and broom, began to gather up the litter. Ruth became very still at the window with the old volume in her lap. The smaller girls were out of the room.

"What's in the old thing—pictures?" asked Agnes of her elder sister.

"Ye—yes, pictures," Ruth said hesitatingly.

"Must be funny ones," chuckled Neale, "by the look of her face."

Ruth did look serious as she sat there, turning the pages of the big, old volume. Had the others noticed particularly they would have seen that the countenance of the oldest Corner House girl had become very pale.

It was so when Mrs. MacCall looked in and said to her: "Oh, Ruth! I do wish you'd come out here and see what that Sammy Pinkney's brought. I dunno whether to laugh, to scream, or to spank him!"

"I'll be there in a moment, Mrs. Mac," Ruth said nervously, jumping up and closing the book.

Then she glanced at Agnes and Neale, seized the volume in her arms, and instead of going out through the butler's pantry after Mrs. MacCall, she crossed the front hall to the sitting room at the rear of the house.

"I like that!" cried Agnes. "Why! I found that old album myself; and I haven't had a chance to look into it yet."

Ruth was only a moment in the sitting room. Then she ran to the kitchen and out upon the cold porch, where Sammy Pinkney, done up in the folds of a huge red comforter like a boa-constrictor suffering from scarlet fever, stood, holding a cage-trap in one mittened hand.

"What do you know about this?" demanded Mrs. MacCall, spectacles on nose and eyeing the contents of the round trap in alarm and disgust.

Uncle Rufus was chuckling hugely in the background. Sandyface, the mother cat, was arching her back and purring pleadingly about Sammy's sturdy legs.

"What are they?" demanded Ruth.

"Mice," grunted Sammy, gruffly. "For Tess' cats. They like 'em, don't they? But my mother says I've got to bring the trap back."

"What's to be done with a boy like that?" demanded Mrs. MacCall. "Being kicked to death with grasshoppers would be mild punishment for him, wouldn't it? What's to be done with eight mice?"

"One kitten will have to go without," said Dot, the literal, as she and Tess joined the party on the porch.

"Come on, now! You gotter let 'em out. I gotter have the trap," was Sammy's gruff statement. He saw that his present was not entirely appreciated by the human members of the Corner House family, whether the feline members approved or not.

"Oh, I'll call the family!" cried Dot, and raised her voice in a shrill cry for "Spotty, Almira, Popocatepetl, Bungle, Starboard, Port, Hard-a-Lee and Mainsheet!" She was breathless when she had finished.

Cats came from all directions. Indeed, they seemed to appear most mysteriously from the ground. Big cats and little cats, black cats and gray cats, striped cats and spotted cats.

"If there were any more of them they'd eat us out of house and home," declared Mrs. MacCall.

"But Almira isn't here!" wailed Dot. "Oh, Ruthie! don't let him open the cage till Almira comes. She wants a chance to catch a mouse."

"I believe you children are little cannibals!" exclaimed the housekeeper. "How can you? Wanting those cats to catch the poor little mice!"

"D'you want 'em for pets?" demanded Sammy, grinning at the housekeeper.

"Ugh! I hate the pests!" cried Mrs. MacCall.

"Do find Almira, Ruthie," begged Dot.

"I gotter take this cage back," said Sammy. "Can't fool here all day with a parcel of girls."

"But Almira—"

But Ruth had gone into the woodshed. She peered into the corners and all around the barrels. Suddenly she heard a cat purring—purring hard, just like a mill!

"Where are you, Almira?" she asked, softly.

"Purr! purr! purr!" went Almira—oh, so loud, and so proudly!

"What is it, Almira?" asked Ruth. "There! I see you—down in that corner. Why, you're on Uncle Rufus' old coat! Oh! What's this?"

The eight mice had been caught by the other cats and killed. Tess came to the woodshed door.

"Oh, Ruth," she asked, "has anything happened to Almira?"

"I should say there had!" laughed the oldest Corner House girl.

"Oh! what is it?" cried Dot, running, too, to see.

"Santa Claus came ahead of time—to Almira, anyway," declared Ruth. "Did you ever see the like? You cunning 'ittle s'ings! Look, children! Four tiny, little, black kittens."

"Oh-oh-ee!" squealed Tess, falling right down on her knees to worship. But Dot looked gravely at the undisturbed Sandyface, rubbing around her feet.

"Goodness me, Sandyface, you're a grandmother!" she said.

CHAPTER V—NO NEWS FOR CHRISTMAS

Almira's addition to the Corner House family was not the only happening which came on this eventful day to fill the minds and the hearts of the Kenway sisters.

Ruth went around with a very serious face, considering the holiday season and all that she and Agnes and Tess and Dot had to make them joyful. Nor was her expression of countenance made any more cheerful by some news bluff Dr. Forsyth gave her when he stopped, while on his afternoon round of calls, to leave four packages marked "Ruth," "Agnes," "Tess" and "Dot."

"Not to be opened till to-morrow, mind," said the doctor. "That's what the wife says. Now, I must hurry on. I've got to go back to the hospital again to-night. I've a bothersome patient there."

"Oh! Not Miss Pepperill?" Ruth cried, for the red-haired school teacher and the matron of the hospital, her sister, were to be the guests of the Corner House girls on the morrow.

Dr. Forsyth took off his hat again and frowned into it. "No," he said, "not her—not now."

"Why, Doctor! what do you mean? Isn't she getting on well?"

"Well? No!" blurted out the physician. "She doesn't please me. She doesn't get back her strength. Her nerves are jumpy. I hear that she was considered a Tartar in the schoolroom. Is that right?"

"Ask Tommy Pinkney," smiled Ruth. "I believe she was considered strict."

"Humph! yes. Short tempered, sharp tongued, children afraid of her, eh?"

"I believe so," admitted Ruth.

"Good reason for that," said the doctor, shaking his head. "Her nerves are worn to a frazzle. I'm not sure that it isn't a teacher's disease. It's prevalent among 'em. The children just wear them out—if they don't take things easily."

"But, Miss Pepperill?"

"I can't get her on her pins again," growled the doctor.

"Oh, Doctor! Can't she come over here with her sister to-morrow?"

"Yes, she'll come in my machine," said the good physician, putting on his hat once more. "What I am talking about is her lack of improvement. She stands still. She makes no perceptible gain. She talks about going back to teaching, and all that. Why, she is no more fit to be a teacher at present than I am fit to be an angel!"

Ruth smiled up at him and patted his burly shoulder. "I am not so sure that you are not an angel, Doctor," she said.

"Yes. That's what they tell me when I've pulled 'em out of trouble by the very scruff of their necks," growled Dr. Forsyth. "Other times, when I am giving them bad tasting medicine, they call me anything but an angel," and he laughed shortly.

"But now—in this case—she's not a bad patient. She can't help her nerves. They have gotten away from her. Out of control. She's not fit to go back to her work—and won't be for a couple of years."

"Oh!" cried Ruth, with pain. She knew what such a thing meant to the two sisters at the hospital. It was really tragic. Mrs. Eland's salary was small, and Miss Pepperill was not the person to wish to be a burden upon her sister. "The poor thing!" Ruth added.

"She ought to have a year—perhaps two—away from all bothersome things," said Dr. Forsyth, preparing to go. "I'd like to have her go away, and her sister with her for a time, to some quiet place, and to a more invigorating climate. And that—well, we doctors can prescribe such medicine for our rich patients only," and Dr. Forsyth went away, shaking his head.

Ruth said nothing to the other girls about this bad report upon Miss Pepperill's condition. They all were interested in Mrs. Eland's sister—more for Mrs. Eland's sake, it must be confessed, than because of any sweetness of disposition that had ever been displayed by the red-haired school teacher.

The two women had lived very unhappy lives. Left orphans at an early age, they were separated, and Miss Pepperill was brought up by people who treated her none too kindly. She was trained as a teacher and had never married; whereas Mrs. Eland was widowed young, had become a nurse, and finally had come to be matron of the Milton Women's and Children's Hospital in the very town where her sister taught school.

The coming together of the sisters, after Miss Pepperill was knocked down by an automobile on the street, seemed quite a romance to the Corner House girls, and they had been vastly interested for some weeks in the affairs of the matron and the school teacher.

The little girls, Tess and Dot, were too much excited over what the eve of Christmas, and the day itself should bring forth, to be much disturbed by even Ruth's grave face.

When they ate dinner that night, in the light of the candles, it seemed as though they ate in a fairy grotto. The big dining room was beautifully trimmed, the lights sparkled upon the newly polished silver and cut glass, a beautiful damask tablecloth was on the board, and the girls in their fresh frocks and ribbons were a delight to the eye.

Dot could not keep her eyes off the open fireplace. Branches of pine had now been set up in the yawning cavern of brick; but plenty of room had been left for the entrance of a Santa Claus of most excellent girth.

"Dot's expecting another Santa—or a burglar—to tumble down the chimney at any moment," laughed Agnes.

"Let us hope he won't be a plumber," said Ruth, smiling gravely. "Another plumber's bill at Christmas would extract all the joy from our festivities."

"Oh! What will Mr. Howbridge say when he sees the bill?" queried Agnes, round-eyed, for she stood somewhat in awe of their very dignified guardian.

"I don't much care what he'll say," said Ruth, recklessly. "Only I wish he were going to be with us to-morrow as he was at Thanksgiving. But he will not be back until long past New Year's."

Before they rose from the table the doorbell began to ring and Uncle Rufus hobbled out to answer it and to receive mysterious packages addressed to the various members of the family. These gifts were heaped in the sitting room, and Tess and Dot were not even allowed a peep at them.

Neale came over and lit up the tree, to the delight of the little girls. The Creamer girls from next door came in to see it, and so did Margaret and Holly Pease from down Willow Street.

Sammy Pinkney had been told he could come; but the red comforter and the hoarse voice had not been for nothing. Mrs. Pinkney sent over word that Sammy had such a cold that she was forced to put him to bed. He was feverish, too; so his Christmas Eve was spent between blankets.

"Oh! I'm so sorry for Sammy," Dot said, feasting her eyes upon the glittering tree. "I know he won't ever see anything so pretty as this."

"Not if he turns pirate, he won't," Tess agreed severely. "I think likely his being sick is a punishment for his saying that there isn't any Santa Claus."

The visiting little girls went home and Tess and Dot were sent off to bed. Not that they were sleepy—oh, no, indeed! They declared that they positively could not sleep—and then were in the Land of Nod almost before their heads touched the pillow.

Ruth kissed them both after she had heard their prayers, and then tiptoed out of the room. Downstairs was suppressed laughter and much running about. Agnes and Neale were beginning to tie the presents on the tree, and to fill the stockings hung on a line across the chimney-place.

Everybody—even Uncle Rufus—had hung up a stocking for Santa Claus to fill with goodies. It had cost infinite labor and urging to get Aunt Sarah to put her stocking in evidence for Kris Kringle; but there it was, a shapeless white affair with unbleached foot and top.

Mrs. MacCall's hung next—rather a natty looking black stocking, if the truth were known—one of a pair, the mate to which had long since been eaten by Billy Bumps, the goat.

Then came the girls' stockings in one-two-three-four order, like a graduated course of bamboo "bells." Then followed one of Neale's golf stockings, which he had brought because it held more than a sock, with Linda's coarse red woollen hose and Uncle Rufus' huge gray yarn sock at the end.

It was great fun to fill the hose and to tie the wonderfully curious packages on the tree and heap them underneath it. Neale was to get all his presents at the Corner House; so that added to the confusion. There was a special corner in the sitting room where Neale's gifts had been hidden; and there he was supposed not to look.

Then Agnes had to go into the kitchen while her presents were being unearthed and properly hung. Last of all, Ruth retired, leaving Agnes and Neale to hang those gifts which the Good Saint had brought the eldest sister. Ruth was tired, for she had worked hard; so she went to sleep and had no idea how long her sister sat up, when Neale went home, or at what hour Mrs. MacCall locked the house and went up to bed.

Agnes and Neale had something besides the hanging of Ruth's presents to interest them. The former found the big, old family album hidden behind the sewing machine in the sitting room. She sat down with Neale to look it over.

CHAPTER VI—TREASURE TROVE

"Why! Did you ever!" gasped Agnes Kenway.

"Thought you said it was a family photograph album!" said Neale O'Neil.

With their heads close together they were looking into the moth-eaten and battered book Agnes had found in the old Corner House garret. On turning the first page a yellowed and time-stained document met their surprised gaze.

There was a picture engraved upon the document, true enough. Such an ornate certificate, or whatever it might be, Agnes or Neale had never even seen before.

"'The Pittsburg & Washington Railroad Co.,'" read Neale, slowly. "Whew! Calls for a thousand dollars—good at any bank."

"Sandbank, I guess it means," giggled Agnes.

But Neale was truly puzzled. "I never saw a bond before, did you, Aggie?"

"A bond! What kind of a bond?"

"Why, the kind this is supposed to be."

"Why, is it a bond?"

"Goodness! you repeat like a parrot," snapped Neale.

"And you're as polite as a—a pirate," declared Agnes.

"Well, did you ever see anything like this?"

"No. And of course, it isn't worth the paper it's printed on. You know very well, Neale, that people don't leave money around—loose—like this!"

"This isn't money; it only calls for money," said the boy.

"I guess it never called very loud for it," giggled Agnes.

"Must be stage money, then," laughed Neale. "Hi! here's more of it."

He had turned a leaf. There was another of the broad, important looking documents pasted in the old book.

"And good for another thousand dollars!" gasped Agnes.

"Phony—phony," chuckled Neale, meaning that the certificates were counterfeit.

"But just see how good they look," Agnes said wistfully.

"And dated more than sixty years ago!" cried Neale. "There were green-goods men in those days, eh? Hello! here's another."

"Why, we're millionaires, Neale," Agnes declared. "Oh! if it were only real we'd have an automobile."

"This is treasure trove, sure enough," her boy chum said.

"What's that?"

"Whatever you find that seems to belong to nobody. I suppose this has been in the garret for ages. Hard for anybody to prove property now."

"But it's not real!"

"Yes—I know. But, if it were—?"

"Oh! if it were!" repeated the girl.

"Wouldn't that be bully?" agreed the boy. But he was puzzling over the mortgage bonds of a railroad which, if it had ever been built at all, was probably now long since in a receiver's hands, and the bonds declared valueless.

"And all for a thousand apiece," Neale muttered, turning the pages of the book and finding more of the documents. "Cracky, Aggie, there's a slew of them."

"But shouldn't they be made out to somebody? Oughtn't somebody's name to be on them?" asked Agnes, thoughtfully.

"No, guess not. These must be unregistered bonds. I expect somebody once thought he was awfully rich with all this paper. It totes up quite a fortune, Aggie."

"Oh, dear!" sighed Agnes. "I guess it's true, Neale: The more you have the more you want. When we were so poor in Bloomingsburg it seemed as though if we had a dollar over at the end of the month, we were rich. Now that we have plenty—all we really need, I s'pose—I wish we were a little bit richer, so that we could have an auto, Neale."

"Uh-huh!" said Neale, still feasting his eyes on the engraved bonds. "Cracky, Aggie! there's fifty of 'em."

"Goodness! Fifty thousand dollars?"

"All in your eye!" grinned Neale. "What do you suppose they ever pasted them into a scrap-book for?"

"That's just it!" cried Agnes.

"What's just it?"

"A scrap-book. I didn't think of it before. They made this old album into a scrap-book."

"Who did?" demanded the boy, curiously.

"Somebody. Children, maybe. Maybe Aunt Sarah Maltby might tell us something about it. And it will be nice for Tess and Dot to play with."

"Huh!" grunted Neale.

"Of course that's it," added the girl, with more assurance. "It's a scrap-book—like a postcard album."

"Huh!" grunted Neale again, still doubtful.

"When Mrs. MacCall was a little girl, she says it was the fad to save advertising cards. She had a big book full."

"Well—mebbe that's it," Neale said grudgingly. "Let's see what else there is in the old thing."

He began to flirt the pages toward the back of the book. "Why!" he exclaimed. "Here's some real stage money. See here!"

"Oh! oh!"

"Doesn't it look good?" said Neale, slowly.

"Just as though it had just come from the bank. What is it—Confederate money, Neale? Eva Larry has a big collection of Confederate bills. Her grandfather brought it home after the Civil War."

"Oh! these aren't Confederate States bills—they're United States bills. Don't you see?" cried Neale.

"Oh, Neale!"

"But you can bet they are counterfeit. Of course they are!"

"Oh, dear!"

"Silly! Good money wouldn't be allowed to lie in a garret the way this was. Somebody'd have found it long ago. Your Uncle Peter, or Unc' Rufus—or somebody. What is puzzling me is why it was put in a scrap-book."

"Oh! they're only pasted in at the corners. There's one all loose. For ten dollars, Neale!"

"Well, you go out and try to spend it, Aggie," chuckled her boy chum. "You'd get arrested and Ruth would have to bail you out."

"It's just awful," Agnes declared, "for folks to make such things to fool other folks."

"It's a crime. I don't know but you can be punished for having the stuff in your possession."

"Goodness me! Then let's put it in the stove."

"Hold on! Let's count it, first," proposed Neale, laughing.

Neale was turning the leaves carefully and counting. Past the tens, the pages were filled with twenty dollar bills. Then came several pages of fifties. Then hundred dollar notes. In one case—which brought a cry of amazement to Agnes' lips—a thousand dollar bill faced them from the middle of a page.

"Oh! goodness to gracious, Neale!" cried the Corner House girl. "What does it mean?"

Neale, with the stub of a pencil, was figuring up the "treasure" on the margin of a page.

"My cracky! look here, Aggie," he cried, as he set down the last figure of the sum. "That's what it is!"

The sum was indeed a fortune. The boy and girl looked at each other, all but speechless. If this were only good money!

"And it's only good for the children to play with," wailed Agnes.

Neale's face grew very red and his eyes flashed. He closed the book fiercely. "If I had so much money," he gasped, "I'd never have to take a cent from Uncle Bill Sorber again as long as I lived, I could pay for my own education—and go to college, too!"

"Oh! Neale! couldn't you? And if it were mine we'd have an auto," repeated Agnes, "and a man to run it."

"Pooh! I could learn to run it for you," proposed Neale. But it was plain by the look on his face that he was not thinking of automobiles.

"Say! don't let's give it to the kids to play with—not yet," he added.

"Why not?"

"I—I don't know," the boy said frankly. "But don't do it. Let me take the book."

"Oh, Neale! you wouldn't try to pass the money?" gasped Agnes.

"Huh! think I'm a chump?" demanded the boy. "I want to study over it. Maybe I'll show the bonds to somebody. Who knows—they may still be of some small value."

"We—ell—of course, the money—"

"That's phony—sure!" cried Neale, hastily. "But bonds sometimes are worth a little, even when they are as old as these."

"No-o," sighed Agnes, shaking her head. "No such good luck."

"But you don't mind if I take the book?" Neale urged.

"No. But do take care of it."

So Neale took the old scrap-book home under his arm, neither he nor Agnes suspecting what trouble and worriment would arise from this simple act.

CHAPTER VII—"GOD REST YE, MERRIE GENTLEMEN"

There was a whisper in the corridor, a patter of softly shod feet upon the stair.

Even Uncle Rufus had not as yet arisen, and it was as black as pitch outside the Corner House windows.

The old dog, Tom Jonah, rose, yawning, from his rug before the kitchen range, walked sedately to the swinging door of the butler's pantry, and put his nose against it. The whispering and pattering of feet was in the front hall, but Tom Jonah's old ears were sharp.

The sounds came nearer. Tess and Dot were coming down to see what Santa Claus had left them. Old Tom Jonah whined, put both paws to the door, and slipped through. He bounded through the second swinging door into the dining room just as the two smallest Corner House girls, with their candle, entered from the hall.

"Oh, Tom Jonah!" cried Tess.

"Merry Christmas, Tom Jonah!" shouted Dot, skipping over to the chimney-place. Then she squealed: "Oh-ee! He did come, Tess! Santa Claus has been here!"

"Well," sighed Tess, thankfully, "it's lucky Tom Jonah didn't bite him."

Dot hurried to move a chair up to the hearth, and climbed upon it to reach her stocking. The tree was in the shadow now, and the children did not note the packages tied to its branches.

Dot unhooked her own and her sister's stockings and then jumped down, a bulky and "knobby" hose under each arm.

"Come on back to bed and see what's in them," proposed Tess.

"No!" gasped Dot. "I can't wait—I really can't, Tess. I just feel as though I should faint."

She dropped right down on the floor, holding her own stocking clasped close to her breast. There her gaze fell upon a shiny, smart-looking go-cart, just big enough for her Alice-doll, that had been standing on the hearth underneath the place where her stocking had hung.

"Oh! oh! OH!" shrieked Dot. "I know I shall faint."

Tess was finding her own treasures; but Tess could never enjoy anything selfishly. She must share her joy with somebody.

"Oh, Dot! Let's show the others what we've got. And Ruthie and Aggie ought to be down, too," she urged.

"Let's take our stockings upstairs and show 'em," Dot agreed.

She piled her toys, helter skelter, into the doll wagon. "My Alice-doll must see this carriage," she murmured, and started for the door. Tess followed with her things gathered into the lap of her robe. Tom Jonah paced solemnly after them, and so the procession mounted the front stairs—Dot having some difficulty with the carriage.

Ruth heard them coming and called out "Merry Christmas!" to them; but Agnes was hard to awaken, for she had been up late. The chattering and laughter finally aroused the beauty, and she sat up in bed, yawning to the full capacity of her "red, red cavern with its fringe of white pearls all around."

"Merry Christmas! Merry Christmas! Merry Christmas!" they all shouted at her.

"Oh—dear—me! Merry Christmas!" returned Agnes. "But why be so noisy about it?"

"Come over here, Miss Lazybones," cried Ruth, "and see what Santa Claus has brought the children."

"What's that?" demanded Agnes, as she hopped out of bed. "Who's going down the back stairs?"

"Linda," said Ruth. "Can't you tell those clod-hopper shoes she wears? I wonder if everybody in Finland wears such footgear?"

"Maybe she's going to look at her stocking," Tess said. "I hope she likes the handkerchiefs I monogrammed for her."

But before long the pungent smell of freshly ground coffee came up the back stairway and assured the girls that the serving maid was at work.

"Why so ear—ear—ear-ly?" yawned Agnes, again. "Why! it's still pitch-dark."

Uncle Rufus was usually the first astir in the Corner House and Linda was not noted for early rising. But now the girls heard the stairs creak again—this time under Mrs. MacCall's firm tread.

"Merry Christmas, Mrs. Mac!" they all shouted.

The smiling Scotchwoman came to the door with her bedroom candle in her hand.

"Indeed, I hope 'twill be a merry ain for my fower sweethearts," she said. "Your Mrs. Mac must have a kiss from ever' ain o' ye," and she proceeded to take toll from the quartette.

"Ye make ma heart glad juist wi' the looks o' ye," she added. "And there's many and many a lonely heart beside mine ma Corner House bairns have made to rejoice. I thank God for ye, ma dearies."

Mrs. MacCall always spoke more broadly when she was moved by sentiment. She wiped her glasses now and prepared to descend to the kitchen when suddenly a chorus of voices broke out below the bedroom windows, in the side yard toward Willow Street.

"Hech, now! what have we here?" cried the housekeeper, going smartly to the window and throwing up the shade and then the sash. The sound poured in—a full chorus of fresh young voices singing a Christmas carol.

"Cover yersel's, ma dearies," advised Mrs. MacCall, "and leesten."

"Oh, oh!" whispered Agnes, fairly hugging herself as she sat upon the bed with her feet drawn up. "It's just as though we lived in a castle—and had a moat and drawbridge and fiefs—"

"Oh," interposed Dot. "That's Mr. Joe Maroni strumming his guitar. I've heard him before."

"Why!" gasped Ruth. "It's the children from Meadow Street."

She ran to the window to peer out. It was a very cold morning, and there was only a narrow band of crimson, pink, and saffron light along the eastern horizon.

She could easily distinguish the sturdy Italian with his guitar which he touched so lightly in accord with the children's voices. There were fully a dozen of the little singers—German and Italian, Jew and Gentile—singing the praise of Christ our Lord in an old Christmas carol.

A bulky figure in the background puzzled Ruth at first; but when a hoarse voice commanded: "Now sing de Christ-childt song—coom! Ein—zwei—drei!" she recognized Mrs. Kranz, the proprietor of the delicatessen store.

The lustily caroling children were some of the Maronis, Sadie Goronofski and her half-brothers and sisters, and other children of the tenants in the Meadow Street property from which the Corner House girls collected rents.

"Oh, my!" murmured Agnes again. "Isn't it great? We ought to throw them largesse—"

"What's that, Aggie?" demanded Dot. "It—it sounds like a kind of cheese. Mr. Maroni sells it."

"No, no!" gasped Tess. "That's gorgonzola—I asked Maria. And—it—smells!"

"Goosey!" laughed Agnes. "Largesse is money. Rich folks used to throw it to the poor."

"My!" observed Dot. "I guess they don't do it now. Poor folks have to work for money."

"It's just dear of them to come and serenade us," Ruth declared. "But it's so cold! Do call them in to get warm, Mrs. Mac."

Already the housekeeper was scurrying downstairs. She had routed out Linda early to make coffee against this very emergency, for Mrs. MacCall had known that the Corner House girls were to be serenaded on Christmas morning.

The four sisters dressed hastily and ran down to greet their little friends from Meadow Street, as well as Mrs. Kranz and Joe Maroni. The latter had brought "the leetla padrona," as he called Ruth, his usual offering of a basket of fruit. Mrs. Kranz kissed the Kenway girls all around, declaring:

"Posies growing de garten in iss nodt so sveet like you kinder. Merry, merry Christmas!"

While the carol singers drank cups of hot coffee the Corner House girls brought forth the presents they had intended to send over to Meadow Street later in the day, but now could give in person to each child.

The choristers went away with merry shouts just at sunrise, and then Dot and Tess insisted that the family should troop into the dining room to take down the rest of the stockings.

Breakfast this morning was a "movable feast" and lasted till nine o'clock. Nobody expected to eat any luncheon; indeed, Mrs. MacCall declared she could not take the time to prepare any.

"You bairns must tak' a 'bit in your fistie,' as we used to say, and be patient till dinner time," she said.

Dinner was to be early. Mrs. Eland and Miss Pepperill came in the doctor's automobile soon after noon, and Tess and Dot were at once engaged in entertaining these guests in the sitting room.

It was a real blessing to the little Corner House girls, for it kept them out of the dining room, where they could not keep their eyes off the heavily laden tree, the fruit of which must not be touched until after dinner.

Neale O'Neil had, of course, come over for his stocking and had expressed his gratitude to his friends at the old Corner House. But, as Ruth had been glum the day before, so Neale was silent now. Agnes became quite angry with him and sent him home in the middle of the forenoon.

"And you needn't come to dinner, sir—nor afterward—if you can't have a Christmas smile upon your face," she told him, severely.

It was while the preparations for dinner were in full progress, that Ruth heard voices on the side porch. Rather, a voice, resonant and commanding which said:

"Hear ye! hear ye! hear ye! I proclaim good tidings to all creatures. Come! gather around me and list to my word. I bear gifts, frankincense and myrrh—"

"Goodness me!" cried Agnes. "That's Seneca Sprague. And look at the cats!"

The girls ran out upon the porch to see a tall, thin, gray-haired man, his abundant hair sweeping his shoulders, dressed in a flapping linen duster and with list slippers on his feet—a queer enough costume indeed for a sharp winter's day. But Seneca Sprague was never more warmly clad than this, and had been known to plod barefooted through snowdrifts.

"Your humble servant, Miss Ruth," said the queer old man, doffing the straw hat and bowing low, for he held the oldest Corner House girl in much deference. "I came to bring you good cheer and wish you a multitude of blessings. Verily, verily, I say unto you, they that give of their substance to the poor shall receive again a thousand fold. May your cup of joy be full to overflowing, Miss Ruth."

"Thank you, Mr. Sprague," replied the girl, gravely, for she made it a rule never to laugh at the "prophet," as he was called, and who people said was demented upon religious subjects.

"Thank you for your good wishes," said Ruth. "And what have you brought the cats?"

For Sandyface and all her progeny had come to meet the prophet and were purring about him and otherwise showing much pleasure. Even Almira had left her young family in the woodshed to come to meet Mr. Seneca Sprague.

From a side pocket of his duster Seneca brought forth a packet. He broke off a little of the pressed herb in the packet and sprinkled it on the stoop. The cats fairly scrambled over each other for a chance to eat some of the catnip, or to roll in it.

They did not quarrel over it. Indeed, the intoxicating qualities of their favorite herb gave the cats quite a Christmas spirit.

Mrs. MacCall brought a shallow pan of milk and some more of the herb was sprinkled in it by the old prophet. The kittens—Starboard, Port, Hard-a-lee and Mainsheet—lapped this up eagerly.

"It's very kind of you to bring the catnip, Mr. Sprague," Ruth said. "Won't you come in and taste Agnes' Christmas cake? She is getting to be a famous cake baker."

"With pleasure," said the queer old man.

After Seneca Sprague's old hut on the river dock was burned at Thanksgiving, and the Corner House girls had found him a room in one of their tenements to live in, he had become a frequent visitor at the old Corner House. Ruth would have ushered him into the sitting room where Mrs. Eland and her sister were; but Seneca shrank from that.

"I am not a society man—nay, verily," quoth the prophet. "The sex does not interest me."

"But it is only Mrs. Eland and her sister, who are our guests to-day for dinner," Ruth said, as she led him into the dining room, while Agnes sped to get the cake.

"Ha! Those Aden girls," said Seneca, referring to the hospital matron and the red-haired school teacher by their family name. "I remember Lemuel Aden well—their uncle. A hard man was Lemuel—a hard man."

"I believe he must have been a very wicked man," declared Agnes, coming back with a generous slice of cake, and overhearing this. "See how he let people think that his brother was dishonest, while he pocketed money belonging to the clients of Mrs. Eland's father. Oh! we know all about it."

"Ah!" said Seneca again, tasting the cake. "Very delicious. I know that you put none of the fat of the accursed swine in your cake as some of these women around here do."

"Lard, he means," whispered Ruth, for Seneca followed the rabbinical laws of the Jews and ate no pork.

"Lemuel Aden was a miser," the prophet announced. "He was worse than your uncle, Peter Stower," he added bluntly. "All three of us went to school together. They were much older than I, of course; but I came here to the Corner House to see Peter at times. And I was here when Lem Aden came last."

"We know about that, too," Agnes said, with some eagerness. "Did—did Uncle Peter really turn him out, and did he wander over into Quoharie Township, and die there in the poorhouse?"

Seneca was silent for a minute, nibbling at the cake thoughtfully. "It comes upon my mind," he said at last, "that Peter Stower was greatly maligned about that matter. Peter was a hard man, but he had soft spots in him. He was a great sinner, in that he ate much meat—which is verily against the commandment. For I say unto you—"

"But how about Mr. Lemuel Aden and Uncle Peter?" interrupted Ruth, gently; for the old prophet was likely to switch off on some foreign topic if not shrewdly guided in his speech.

"Ah! Lemuel Aden came back here to Milton when he was an old man. Not so old in years, perhaps; but old in wickedness, and aged beyond his years by his own miserliness. We had heard he was rich, but he declared he had nothing—had lost everything in speculation; and he said all he possessed was in the old carpetbag he brought.

"Peter Stower took him in," Seneca continued. "But Lemuel was a dirty old man and made that colored man a lot of trouble. It was thought by everybody that Lemuel Aden had even more wealth than Peter Stower; but nobody ever knew of his spending a penny. Peter said he had money; and so finally turned him out."

"How long did he stay here at the old Corner House?" asked Ruth.

"Verily he would have remained until his end; but Peter became angry with him and threatened to hand him over to the town authorities. They quarreled harshly—I was here at the time. The colored man must have heard much of the quarrel, too," Seneca proceeded.

"I went away in the midst of it. Peace dwelleth with me—yea, verily. I am not a man of wrath. Later I learned that Lemuel Aden went away cursing Peter Stower, and he was never more seen again in Milton."

"But was he poor?" Ruth asked. "Did Uncle Peter turn him out to suffer?"

Seneca Sprague shook his head. "Nay; I would not charge that to Peter Stower's account," he said. "It was believed by everybody, as I say, that Lemuel had much money hidden away. Peter Stower said he knew it."

"Just the same, he died in the Quoharie poorhouse," Agnes cried, quickly.

"He would have been cared for here in Milton by the authorities had he asked help. Peter Stower and Lemuel Aden were both misers. It was said of them that each had the first dollar he ever earned."

"Dear me!" Ruth said, as the old prophet concluded. "If Mr. Aden did have money at any time, it is too bad Mrs. Eland can't find it. She and her sister need it now, if ever they did," and she sighed, thinking of Dr. Forsyth's report upon Miss Pepperill's condition.

CHAPTER VIII—WHERE IS NEALE O'NEIL?

Christmas Day wore away toward evening. A number of the young friends of the Corner House girls ran in to bring gifts and to wish Ruth and Agnes and Tess and Dot a Merry Christmas. Many of them, too, stayed for a moment to speak to Mrs. Eland and Miss Pepperill. The interest aroused by the recently performed play at the Opera House for the benefit of the Women's and Children's Hospital had awakened interest likewise in "the little gray lady" and her sister.

"I never was so popular before with the school children of Milton," the latter said, rather tartly. "I'd better be run down by an automobile about once a year."

"Oh, that would be dreadful!" Tess exclaimed.

"It is a shame you don't know who it was that ran you down. He could be made to pay something," Ruth remarked.

"My goodness! Get money that I hadn't earned!" cried the school teacher.

"I should say you'd earned it—and earned it mighty hard," said Mrs. MacCall, who happened to hear this.

"It wouldn't be my fortune," said Miss Pepperill, lying back wearily in her chair. "And I don't see how I can go back to those awful youngsters after New Year."

"Sh!" begged Mrs. Eland.

"Oh, my! is our Tess an awful youngster?" asked Dot, bluntly.

"She is a dear!" declared Mrs. Eland, quickly.

"Theresa is an exception," admitted Miss Pepperill. "But I certainly have some little tikes in my room."

"Oh, I know," said Dot. "Like Sammy Pinkney."

"Sammy's sick abed," Tess said, coming into the room in time to hear his name mentioned. "I went over and asked his mother about him. The doctor won't say what it is yet; but he's out of his head."

"Poor Sammy!" said Agnes. "Falling down our chimney yesterday was too much for him. He's an unfortunate little chap after all."

"Oh, my!" Dot observed, "if he is sick and dies, he'll never get to be a pirate, will he?"

"Hear that child!" murmured Miss Pepperill, eyeing Dot as though she were a strange specimen indeed.

"Don't speak so, Dottie," admonished Tess. "That would be dreadful!"

"What? Dreadful if he didn't get to be a pirate?" Agnes asked lightly.

But Tess was serious. "I don't believe Sammy Pinkney is fit to die," she declared.

"For pity's sake!" exclaimed Miss Pepperill. "She talks like her grandmother. I never heard such a child as you are, Theresa. But perhaps you are right about Sammy. He's one awful trial."

"But his mother was crying," said Tess, softly.

Nobody said anything more to the tender-hearted little girl; but Dot brought her the nicest piece of "Christmas" candy in the dish—a long, curly, striped piece, and Agnes hugged her.

Ruth was worried a little about the dinner arrangements. The meal was almost ready to serve, but Neale O'Neil had not come over from Mr. Con Murphy's, where he lived.

"You were cross with him, Agnes, and he won't come back," she said accusingly to the beauty. "And Mrs. MacCall won't wait."

"Oh, he wouldn't disappoint us!" declared Agnes. "He knows we depend on him. Why, half our fun will be spoiled—"

"He evidently isn't coming to dinner."

At that moment Uncle Rufus came to announce that all was ready, and he tucked a twist of paper into Agnes' hand.

"Oh, Ruthie! look here!" the second sister said. "Read this."

The oldest Corner House girl saw it was the handwriting of their boy friend.

"'Don't worry. Santa Claus will appear according to schedule.' Oh! that is all right, then," Ruth said. "He's not coming till after we get through."

"Well! I think that's too mean of him," cried Agnes.

But Ruth was somewhat relieved. They went in to dinner, a quiet, but really happy party.

The old dining room looked lovely, and the lighted tree in the corner was a brilliant spectacle. Ruth's idea of lighting the room completely by candles proved a good one. The soft glow of the wax-lights over the ancient silver and sparkling cut-glass was attractive.

Mrs. MacCall presided, as always. The girls would not hear to her only directing the dinner from the kitchen. Aunt Sarah Maltby, in her best black silk and ivory lace, seemed to have imbibed a share of the holiday spirit, for once at least. She was quite talkative and gracious at the other end of the table.

Without Neale O'Neil, Ruth found that the table could be much better balanced. Mrs. Eland sat between Tess and Dot on one side of the long board, while Miss Pepperill's place was between the two older Corner House girls.

Uncle Rufus came in chuckling toward the close of the meal and whispered something to Ruth. Almost immediately she excused Tess and Dot to run up for their dolls. The presents were to be taken off the tree and there might be some for the Alice-doll and Tess' most treasured doll, too.

When the little folks returned something had disturbed the green boughs in the chimney-place. Dot had only begun to eye that place of mystery with growing curiosity, when there was a shaking of the branches, two mighty thumps upon the brick hearth, and pushing through the greenery came Santa Claus himself.

"Merry Christmas! And the best of iv'rything to ye!" cried the good saint jovially.

"Oh, my!" gasped Dot. "Is—is it the really truly Santa Claus?"

"I don't believe that Santa is Irish," whispered Tess. "This is just in fun!" But she could not imagine, any more than did Dot, who it was behind the mask and great paunch that disguised the Santa Claus.

They all hailed him merrily, however. Even Miss Pepperill and Aunt Sarah entered into the play to a degree. Santa Claus went to the tree and they all sat along the opposite side of the cleared table, facing him. With many a quip and jest he brought the packages and presented them to those whose names were written on the wrappers. At one place quite a little pile of presents were gathered, all addressed to Neale O'Neil.

"Oh, dear me!" sighed Tess, almost overcome with joy, yet thinking of the absent one. "If Neale were only here! I do so want to see how he likes his presents."

But Neale did not come. The two little girls finally tripped up to bed with their arms full. Then the party broke up and the masquerading Santa Claus took off his paunch and false face in the kitchen.

"Shure I promised the lad I'd do it for him," said Mr. Con Murphy, accepting a piece of Agnes' cake and sitting down to enjoy it. "No, he's not mad wid yez. Shure not!"

"But why didn't he come to dinner?" demanded Agnes, quickly.

"He ain't here," said the cobbler, quietly. "He's gone away."

"Do you mean he's gone away from your house?" asked Ruth, curiously, for Agnes was too much surprised to speak.

"Shure, he's gone away from Milton entirely," said the little Irishman.

"What for?" demanded both girls together.

"Begorra! he didn't say, now," said Mr. Murphy, slowly. "Come to think of ut, he niver told me. But I knowed the letter puzzled him."

"What letter?" asked Ruth.

"He never told me he got a letter," cried Agnes, much put out.

"It was there last evening when he got home. The postman brought it jest before supper," said Mr. Murphy, reflectively. "Ye, see, Neale was over here all the evening and shure, he didn't see the letter till he come home."

"Oh!" was the chorused exclamation.

"I see he was troubled in his mind this mornin'," said the cobbler. "'What's atin' on yer mind, lad?' says I to him. But niver a wor'd did he reply to me till afther he'd been over here and come back again. Then he came downstairs with his bist clo'es on and his bag in his hand."

"For pity's sake!" wailed Agnes, "where has he gone?"

"He didn't say," returned the old Irishman, shaking his head. "Neale can be as tight-mouthed as a clam—so he can."

"But he did not go off without saying a word to you?" cried Ruth.

"No, not so. He says: 'Con, I've gotter go. 'Tis me duty. I hate mesilf for going; but I'd hate meself worse if I didn't go.' Now! kin ye make head nor tail of that? For shure, I can't," finished the cobbler.

The two Corner House girls stared at each other. Neither of them could see into this mystery any deeper than did Mr. Con Murphy.

CHAPTER IX—RUTH IS SUSPICIOUS

The day following Christmas Ruth went out of her way while she was marketing to step into the bank in which Mr. Howbridge kept their account, and where she was known to both the cashier and teller.

"Good morning, Mr. Crouch," she said to the latter gentleman. "Will you look at this bill?"

"Merry Christmas to you, Miss Ruth," said the teller. "What is the matter with the bill?" and he took the one she tendered him.

"Perhaps you can tell me better than I can tell you," Ruth returned, laughing; yet she looked a bit anxious, too, and her hand trembled.

"Has somebody been giving you a 'phony' ten dollar note?" asked the teller, taking up his glass and screwing it into his eye.

"I am not sure," replied Ruth, hesitatingly.

"Or is it a Christmas present and you are looking a gift horse in the mouth?" and Mr. Crouch chuckled as he bent above the banknote. "This appears to be all right. Do you want it broken—or changed for another note?"

"No-o. I guess not. I only wanted to be sure," Ruth said. "Of course you can't be mistaken, Mr. Crouch?"

"Mistaken? Of course I can," he cried. "Did you ever hear of a mere human who wasn't sometimes mistaken?" and he laughed again.

"About that being a good bill, I mean," she said, trying to laugh with him.

"I'm so sure that I'm willing to exchange good money for it," he said, with confidence. "I can say no more than that."

Ruth gravely folded the bill again and tucked it into one compartment of her purse, by itself. She looked very serious all the way home with her laden basket.

While the eldest Corner House girl was absent Tess and Dot had been very busy in their small way. Life was so "full of a number of things" for the two smallest Corner House girls that they were seldom at a loss for something to do.

First of all that morning Tess insisted upon calling at the Pinkneys' side door to ask after Sammy. She felt it her duty, she said.

When they approached the porch Dot's quick eyes caught sight of a brilliantly red card, about four inches square, tacked to the post.

"What do you suppose that is, Tess Kenway?" she demanded, stopping short.

"Goodness! what does it say?" responded Tess, puzzled for the moment.

"Why! it looks just like what was tacked on the front door of the Creamers' house when Mabel's sisters had quarantine. Don't you 'member?" demanded Dot.

"Oh, dear me!" cried Tess. "It's scarlet fever. Then Sammy's really got it!"

"Is—is it catching?" asked Dot, backing away and hugging tighter her Alice-doll, which she had snatched out of the carriage.

"I—guess—so," said Tess. "Oh, poor Sammy!"

"Do you 'spect he'll die?" asked Dot, in awed tone.

"Oh, goodness me! I don't know!" exclaimed Tess.

"And won't he ever grow up to be a pirate?" queried Dot, for to the mind of the smallest Corner House girl romance gilded Sammy Pinkney's proposed career.

"Scarlet fever's dreadful bad. And we mustn't go in," Tess said.

"I'm sorry for Sammy," observed Dot. "I think he's a terrible int'resting boy."

"You shouldn't be interested in the boys," declared prudish Tess.

"Huh! you wanted to come here to see how he was," responded the smallest Corner House girl, shrewdly.

"But I don't think of him as a boy. I'm just sorry for him 'cause he's a human being," declared Tess, loftily.

"Oh!"

"I'd be sorry for anybody who had scarlet fever."

"Well," Dot said, rather weary of the subject, "let's go over to see Mabel Creamer. Now we're out with our doll carriages, we ought to call somewhere."

Tess agreed to this and the little girls wheeled their baby carriages around the corner to their next door neighbor's, on the other side of the old Corner House.

The Creamer cottage seemed wonderfully quiet and deserted in appearance as they went in at the gate and pushed their doll carriages up to the side porch.

"Do you s'pose they're all away?" worried Tess.

"Maybe they've got the scarlet fever, too," murmured Dot, in awe.

But just then a figure appeared at the sitting room window which, on spying the Corner House girls, began to jump up and down and make urgent gestures for them to come in.

"It's Mabel," said Tess. "And she must be all alone."

"Oh, goody! then her sisters can't boss us," cried Dot, hurrying to drag her Alice-doll's new go-cart up the steps.

Mabel, the Creamer girl nearest the little Kenways' own ages, ran to open the door.

"Oh, hurrah!" she cried. "Come in, do! Tess and Dot Kenway. I'm so lonesome I could kill flies! Dear me! how glad I am to see you," and she hugged them both and then danced around them again.

"Are you all alone, Mabel?" asked Dot, struggling with her hood and coat in the warm hall.

"Well, Minnie" (that was the maid's name) "has just run down to the store. She won't be gone long. But I might as well be all alone. Mother's gone to Aunt Em's and Lydia's taken Peg to have a tooth pulled."

"But the baby?" asked Tess. "Didn't I just hear him?"

"Oh, yes," said Mabel, scowling. "I've got to mind the baby. I told Lydia I'd go have a tooth pulled and Peg could mind him. I'd rather."

"Oh!" cried Dot, in awe, while Tess marched straight into the sitting room to see if the Creamers' youngest was all right.

"You don't deserve to have a baby brother, Mabel Creamer," Tess said severely.

"Oh, I wish we could have one!" Dot said longingly.

"Say! you can have this one for all I care," declared Mabel. "You don't know what a nuisance babies are. Everybody else can go out but me. I've got to stay and mind the baby. Nasty thing!"

"Oh, Mabel!" said Tess, sorrowfully—for Tess had no objection to boys as small as Bubby Creamer. The baby laughed, and crowed, and stretched out his arms to her. "Isn't he the cunning little thing, Dot?" cooed Tess.

"He's the nicest baby I ever saw," agreed the smallest Corner House girl.

"Oh, yes," growled Mabel, who had been the baby in the family herself for a long time before Bubby came. "Oh, yes, he's so cunning! Look at him now— trying to get his foot in his mouth. If I bite my fingernails mother raps me good; but that kid can swallow his whole foot and they think he's cute!"

"Oh, Mabel! does he really swallow his foot?" gasped Dot. "I should think it would choke him."

"Wish it would!" declared the savage sister of the cooing Bubby Creamer. "Then I could get out and play once in a while. Lydia and Peg put it on me, anyway. They get the best of everything."

"Oh, let's play right here," suggested Tess, interrupting this ill-natured tirade. "You get your new doll, Mabel."

"No. If I do he'll want it. See! he's trying to grab your Alice-doll right now, Dot Kenway."

"Oh! he can't have her," Dot gasped, in alarm. "Haven't you an old dolly you can let him play with, Mabel?"

"He's got one of his own—a black boy. As black as your Uncle Rufus. I'll hunt around for it," said the ungracious Mabel.

Afterward, when the little Kenways were on their way home, after bidding Mabel and Bubby good-bye, Dot confessed to her sister:

"I don't so much like to go to see Mabel Creamer, after all. She's always so scoldy."

"I know," agreed Tess. "And she's real inquisitive, too. Did you hear her asking 'bout Neale?"

"I didn't notice," Dot said.

"Why, she says they saw Neale O'Neil going through our yard with a heavy traveling bag yesterday morning, and he went out our front gate. She asked where he was going."

"But you don't know where Neale has gone," said Dot, complacently, "so she didn't find out anything. And I'd like to know where he's gone, too. There's all his presents off the Christmas tree; and we can't see them till he comes back, Ruthie says."

More than Dot expressed a desire to see Neale at the old Corner House. Agnes had gone about all the morning openly wondering where Neale could have gone, and what he had gone for.

"I think he's just too mean for anything," she said to Ruth, querulously, when the older girl came home from market.

"Who is mean?" Ruth returned absently.

"Neale. To go off and never say a word to us. I am offended."

Had Agnes' mind not been so strongly set upon the subject of Neale O'Neil's defection she would surely have noticed how Ruth's hands trembled and how her face flushed and paled by turns.

"Never mind about Neale O'Neil," the older sister said, rather impatiently for her.

"Well, I just do mind!" Agnes declared. "He has no business to have secrets from us. Aren't we his best friends?"

"Perhaps he doesn't consider us such," said Ruth, who would have been amused by her sister's seriousness at another time. "There's Joe Eldred. Perhaps he knows where Neale has gone."

"Joe Eldred!" cried Agnes. "If I thought Neale had taken a mere boy into his confidence and hadn't told me, I'd never speak to him again! At least," she temporized, knowing her own failing, "I never would forgive him!"

"Never mind worrying about Neale," Ruth said again. "Come into the sitting room. I want to show you something."

Agnes followed her rather grumpily. To her mind there was nothing just then so important as Neale O'Neil's absence and the mystery thereof.

Ruth turned to her when the door was closed and started to open her purse and her lips at the same time. Her eyes sparkled; her cheeks were deeply flushed. She looked just as eager and excited as ever quiet, composed Ruth Kenway could look.

"Oh, Aggie!" she quavered.

"Well!" said Agnes, querulously. "I don't care. He—"

"Never mind Neale O'Neil!" cried Ruth, for a third time, and quite exasperated with her sister.

She closed her purse again and ran across the room. She looked behind the machine. Then she pulled the machine away from the wall so that she could get down on her knees and creep behind it.

"What's the matter with you, Ruthie?" asked Agnes, finally awakening to her sister's strange behavior. "What are you looking for?"

"Where—where is it? Where has it gone?" gasped Ruth, still on hands and knees.

"What are you after, Ruth Kenway?" cried Agnes again. "Oh! are you looking for that old scrap-book I found upstairs in the garret?"

"Yes," answered Ruth, quaveringly.

"Why? Did you see what was in it?" demanded her sister.

"Yes," Ruth said again.

"Wasn't it funny? All that counterfeit money and those old bonds. Neale and I looked at it Christmas Eve."

"Neale?" gasped Ruth, getting upon her feet, but sitting down in a chair quickly as though her knees were too weak to bear her up.

"Oh, dear me!" rattled on Agnes. "Wouldn't it have been great if the money and bonds were good? Why! it would have been a fortune. Neale added it all up."

"But what became of the book?" Ruth finally got a chance to ask again.

"Oh! Neale took it."

"Neale took it?"

"Yes."

"What for?"

"Why, I don't know. He was curious. He said maybe the bonds were worth something and he'd find out. Of course, that is silly," said Agnes, lightly, "and I told him so."

"And didn't he bring all that money back?" gasped Ruth.

"'All that money,'" repeated Agnes, with laughter. "How tragic you sound—just as though it were not stage money. And I wish it were not!"

"He—he didn't return the book?" asked Ruth, controlling herself with difficulty.

"Not yet. He went away so suddenly. Mean thing! I'd just like to know where he's gone."

Agnes was quite unaware of her sister's trouble. Her own mind reverted to Neale's strange absence as of more importance. Ruth began to be troubled by that same query, too. Where was Neale O'Neil? And what had he done with the old album found in the Corner House garret?

The ten dollar bill Ruth had had examined at the bank that morning was one she had taken out of the old volume!

CHAPTER X—WHAT MR. CON MURPHY DID NOT KNOW

The children saw Dr. Forsyth coming out of Sammy Pinkney's house that afternoon and they ran to ask him how their neighbor was getting on.

"For we're awful int'rested in Sammy," Dot explained. "I'm int'rested because he's going to be a pirate, and Tess is int'rested because he gave her a goat."

"You children stay across the street where you are," commanded the busy doctor, getting briskly into his automobile. "You're quite near enough to me. This is my last call and I'm going home now to fumigate my clothing."

"Oh, dear me!" cried Dot, "has Sammy scarlet fever and quarantine, both?"

"Huh?" said the doctor, trying his starter. Then he laughed. "I should say he had. And you children must stay away from there. It's bad enough to have one scarlet fever patient on Willow Street. I don't want an epidemic."

That last puzzled Dot a good deal. She went back into the house very soberly when the doctor drove away.

"Mrs. MacCall," she asked, "what is a epidermis? Dr. Forsyth doesn't want one."

"Well, that's 'no skin off your nose,' Dot," said Agnes, giggling at her own fun.

"If the doctor had no epidermis he'd be a rare lookin' object," said the housekeeper, "for that's his skin, just as your sister says."

"He said 'epidemic,'" Tess declared, with disgust. "Dot! you do make the greatest mistakes."

"Well, has Sammy got that too?" cried Dot, horrified by the possibility of such a complication of diseases. "Has he got scarlet fever, and quarantine, and ep— epic—well, that other thing, too?"

Ruth came through the kitchen dressed to go out. Her face was very grave and her eyes suspiciously red; but she pulled her veil down over her face and so hid the traces of her emotion from the family.

"Where are you going, Ruthie?" asked Dot, eagerly.

"Sister's going out on an errand," replied Ruth.

"Oh! let me go?" cried the smallest Corner House girl.

"Not this time," said Ruth, quietly. "I can't take you to-day, Dot."

Dot began to pout. "Oh, come along, Dot," said Tess, who never could bear to see her little sister with a frown. "Let us go upstairs and dress all the dolls in their best clothes, and have a party."

"No," said Dot. "I can't. Muriel has spoiled her party dress. She spilled tea on it, you know. Bonnie-Betty's broken her arm and it's in splints. And you know Ann Eliza and Eliza Ann, the twins, are all spotted up, and I don't know yet whether it's measles or smallpox."

"For goodness' sake!" gasped Mrs. MacCall. "If they need a quarantine anywhere I should think 'twould be in that nursery."

Ruth went out, leaving them all laughing at Dorothy. She was in no mood for laughter herself. Since she and her sisters had come to live at the old Corner House, Ruth had never felt more troubled.

She said nothing further to Agnes either about the absence of Neale O'Neil, or the disappearance of the old album. The next to the oldest Corner House girl had noted nothing strange in Ruth's manner or speech. Agnes Kenway was not very observant.

Ruth went out the side gate and along Willow Street. Beyond Mrs. Adam's little cottage there was a narrow lane called Willow Wythe, which ran back, in a sort of L-shaped passage to the rear street on which Mr. Con Murphy had his tiny house and shop.

Neale always came to the Corner House by a 'short cut'—over the fence into the back premises from Mr. Murphy's yard; and Agnes had been known to come and go by the same route. It was several minutes' walk by way of Willow Street and Willow Wythe to the door of the cobbler's little shop.

Neale O'Neil had lived here with Mr. Murphy, occupying an upstairs room, almost ever since he had come to Milton to go to school. Mr. Murphy's pig had served as an introduction between Neale and the cobbler. Mr. Murphy always thought a good deal of his pig. Later he thought so much of Neale that he offered to buy the boy's services from his Uncle Bill Sorber, when that gentleman had tried to take Neale back to the circus.

"Shure," Mr. Murphy had said, "there's more to a bye than to a pig, afther all—though there's much to be said in favor of the pig, by the same token!"

However, either the cobbler's generosity, or something else, had shamed Mr. Sorber into agreeing to let Neale have his chance for an education; and he was willing to pay the boy's expenses while he went to school, too. But Neale worked hard to help support himself, for he disliked being a burden on his uncle.

The old cobbler was a queer character, but with a heart of gold. He tapped away all day at the broken footgear of all the neighbors, ever ready for a bit of gossip, yet exuding a kindly philosophy all his own in dealing with neighborhood topics, or human frailties in general.

"There's so little good in the best of us, and so little bad in the worst of us, that it behooves the most of us to take care how we speak ill of the rest of us," was the sum and substance of Mr. Con Murphy's creed.

"Happy the day when yer shadder falls across the threshold, Miss Ruth," was the Irishman's greeting as she pushed inward the door of his shop which was in what had been the parlor of the tiny house. "Bless yer swate face! what's needed?"

"We want to know what's become of Neale, Mr. Murphy," said Ruth, sitting down in the customer's chair.

"Shure, miss, as I told ye, I'd like to l'arn that same meself."

"You have no idea where he's gone?"

"Not the laist. He give me no warnin' that he was thinkin' of goin' till he walked downstairs, wid the travelin' bag in his hand, and bade me good-bye."

"And he said nothing about where he was going?"

"Not a wor-rd."

"Nor how long he would stay?"

"Not a wor-rd."

"Well!" cried Ruth, with some vigor, "it is the strangest thing! How could he act so? And you have been so kind to him!"

"He was troubled in his mind, Miss Ruth. I kin see you are troubled in yours. Kin old Con help ye?" asked the cobbler, shrewdly.

"I don't know," Ruth said, all of a flutter. "I am dreadfully anxious about Neale O'Neil's going away so abruptly."

"He's a smart boy for his age. He'll get into no trouble, I belave."

"I'm not so much disturbed by that thought," admitted Ruth. "I am really selfish. I want to see him. Agnes let Neale take something we found in our garret, on Christmas Eve, and—and—well, it's something valuable, I believe, and I must show it to Mr. Howbridge as soon as possible."

"Something vallible, is ut?" observed Mr. Murphy, with his head on one side.

"I—I have reason to believe so," replied Ruth, with hesitation.

"What is it?" was the cobbler's direct question.

"A—a sort of scrap-book. An old album. A big, heavy book, Mr. Murphy. Oh! it doesn't seem possible that Neale would have taken it away. Have you seen it anywhere about, sir?"

"He brought it home Christmas Eve, ye say?" was the noncommittal reply.

"That is when Agnes let him have it—yes," said the girl, earnestly.

"I did not see him when he came home that night. I was abed. I told ye he got a letter. I left it on his bureau when I went to me own bed. Shure, he might have brought in an elephant for all I'd knowed about it afther I got to sleep," declared the cobbler, shaking his head. "Old Murphy-us himself, him as was the god of sleep, niver slept sounder nor me, Miss Ruth. He must have been the father of all us Murphies, for we were all sound sleepers, praise the pigs!"

"Perhaps the book is in his room," Ruth said, with final desperation.

"A big book, is ut?"

"Oh, yes, sir. Have you seen it?"

"I have not. But I'll go up and look for ut this instant," Mr. Murphy said, rising briskly.

Ruth told him carefully what to look for—as far as the outside of the volume appeared. She devoutly hoped he would not be curious enough to open it.

For no matter who really owned the old album—and to whom its wonderful contents would be finally awarded—the oldest Corner House girl felt herself to be responsible for the safety of the book and its contents. How it came in the garret, why it was hidden there, and who now had the first right to it, she did not know; but Ruth was sure that the odd find was of great value and that it would be a temptation to almost anybody.

Neale might have gone away for an entirely different reason; yet he had the treasure trove in his possession last, and Ruth would not feel relieved until she had recovered it.

In five minutes Con came downstairs again, but without the book.

"I seen nawthin' of the kind," he said. "But here's the envelope of the letter he resaved."

He handed it to Ruth. The address was written by a hand that certainly was not used to holding a pen. The scarcely decipherable address was to "Mist. Nele O. Sorber."

"Shure the postman skurce knew whether to bring it here, or no," Mr. Murphy explained.

"I—I would like to take this," Ruth said slowly.

"Shure ye may. I brought it down ter ye," said Mr. Murphy, taking up his hammer once more.

"But where do you suppose he could have put that book of ours?" Ruth asked, faintly.

"Shure, ma'am, I dunno. Would he be takin' it away wid him to read?"

"Oh, but could he?" gasped Ruth. "It was heavy."

"So was his bag heavy. I knowed by the way he carried it. And I see it's few of his clo'es he took, by the same token, for they are all hangin' in his closet, save the ones he's got on."

Ruth's thoughts fairly terrified her. She got up and was scarcely able to thank Mr. Murphy. She had to get out into the air and recover her self-control.

Neale! The boy whom they had befriended and helped and trusted! Under temptation, Neale had fallen!

For Ruth knew well how the ex-circus boy disliked taking money from his Uncle Bill Sorber, or being beholden to him in any way. Neale worked hard— very hard indeed for a boy of his age—in order to use as little as possible of Mr. Sorber's money.

Sorber held Neale's long-lost father in light repute, and could not understand the boy's desiring an education and wishing to be something besides a circus performer. To the mind of the old circus man it was an honor to be connected with such an aggregation as Twomley & Sorber's Herculean Circus and Menagerie. And Neale's father had left the company years before in search of a better fortune.

Ruth's mind was filled with suspicion regarding Neale now. Knowing his longing for independence, why should she not believe that seeing a chance to obtain a great sum of money with no effort at all he had fallen before the temptation and run away with the old album and its wonderful contents?

Ruth knew there was a fortune in that old and shabby volume which must have lain long in the garret of the old Corner House. If one of the notes was good, why not all the others—and the bonds, too?

She opened her purse and withdrew the folded ten-dollar bill. At the same moment another banknote fell to the ground—another of the same denomination.

"Oh!" she said aloud. "That's the bill Mr. Howbridge gave me when he went away, saying I might need something extra."

She picked it up. It was folded exactly like the other one; but it never entered Ruth's mind that she might have handed Mr. Crouch the wrong bill to examine.

Ruth replaced the banknotes in her purse and walked home with a face still troubled. She could take nobody into her confidence—least of all Agnes— regarding the missing album. It might be, of course, that Neale O'Neil had only hidden away the old book until his return. Possibly it was perfectly safe, and

Neale O'Neil might have no more idea that the money was good than had Agnes.

But oh! if Mr. Howbridge were only at home! That was the burden of Ruth's troubled thought.

She went into the house, her return not being remarked by the younger children. Upstairs Agnes was at her dresser putting the finishing touches to her hair and her frock in readiness for dinner.

"What's that?" she asked Ruth, as the latter put down her purse and likewise the torn envelope Mr. Con Murphy had given her.

"Oh!" ejaculated Ruth. "I must have brought it away with me."

"Brought what away with you—and from where?" demanded Agnes, picking up the paper. Then in a moment she cried: "Why! it's addressed to Neale—by his circus name, 'Neale Sorber.' Where'd you get it, Ruth?"

"I saw Mr. Murphy," the older sister confessed. "He thinks that the letter that came in this envelope was the cause of Neale's going away so suddenly."

"Goodness! it's some trouble about his uncle," said Agnes. "How Neale hates to be called 'Sorber,' too!"

"That isn't his uncle's writing," Ruth said.

"Of course it isn't," the second sister replied scornfully. "Mr. Bill Sorber doesn't write at all. Don't you remember? That's why he thinks it so foolish for Neale to want an education. But it's somebody Uncle Bill's got to write for him."

Agnes' practical explanation could not be gainsaid. She did not connect for a moment the disappearance of the old album with Neale's sudden flight from Milton. The bonds and banknotes pasted into the big volume she had found in the garret gave Agnes not the least anxiety. But she looked closely at the envelope.

"Wish Mr. Murphy had found the letter, too," she said. "Then we could have learned what made that horrid boy run off so."

"'Tiverton,' Humph! Where's Tiverton? That's where this letter was mailed. Seems to me somebody said 'Tiverton' to me only lately," murmured Agnes.

Ruth did not hear her, and Agnes said no more about it. But after she had retired that night and was almost in dreamland—in that state 'twixt waking and sleeping when the happenings of the day pass through one's mind in seemingly endless procession—suddenly Agnes sat up in bed.

"Oh! I know where I've heard of Tiverton before," she whispered shrilly in the darkness. "That's where Mr. Howbridge has gone—to see his sick brother. Say, Ruth!"

Ruth was asleep. And by morning Agnes had forgotten all about the matter. So the coincidence was not called to the older sister's attention.

CHAPTER XI—SOME EXCITEMENT

As Uncle Rufus had stated, his daughter, the pleasant and unctious Petunia Blossom, was to take a week's vacation from laundry work at New Year's; but she brought the last wash home a few days after Christmas.

Petunia was very, very black, and monstrous fat! Her father often mournfully wondered "huccome she so brack," when he was only mahogany brown himself and Petunia's mother had been "light favahed," too.

"Nevah did see the lak' ob her color," declared Uncle Rufus, shaking his grizzled head. "W'en she was a baby we couldn't fin' her in de dark, 'ceptin' her eyes was open, or she was a-bellerin'."

The Corner House girls all liked Petunia Blossom, and her family of cunning piccaninnies. There was always a baby, and in naming her numerous progeny she had secured the help of her white customers, some of whom were wags, as witness a portion of the roll-call of the younger Blossoms:

"Ya'as'm, Miss Tessie. Alfredia's home takin' car' ob de baby. Burne-Jones W'istler—he de artis' lady named—an' Jackson Montgomery Simms, done gone tuh pick up wood, where dey is buildin' dat new row ob flats. Gladiola, she's jes' big nuff now tuh mess intuh things. I tol' Alfredia to keep an eye on Glad."

"That's a pretty name," said Agnes, who heard this; "Gladiola. I hope you'll find as pretty a name for the baby."

"I has, Miss Aggie," Petunia assured her.

"Oh! but that would be hard. He's a boy. You can't name him after a flower, as you did little Glad and Hyacinth and Pansy."

"Oh, ya-as'm," Petunia said, with confidence. "I done hit. De baby, he named aftah a flower, too. I named him 'Artuhficial,' an' we calls him 'Arty' fo' short."

"Oh, my dear! 'Artificial' flower—of course!" gasped Agnes, and ran away to have her laugh out. It certainly pleased the Corner House family. But Uncle Rufus was critical as usual:

"Sho' don't see why de good Lawd send all dem bressed babies t' dat no-'count brack woman. He must know dey ain't a-gettin' no fittin' care. Why—see yere! She don't know how even t' name 'em propah. Flower names—indeedy, das jes' mak' me powerful squeegenny, das does—sho' nuff! Ain't dey no sensible names lef' in dis worl', Ah'd lak't' know?"

There was nobody able to answer Uncle Rufus' question, and he went away, grumbling to himself. And, as he was not within call later, that was why Dot chanced to go to the drug store for Mrs. MacCall, who could not wait for the old colored man's return.

Tess was upstairs helping Agnes make the beds. Mrs. MacCall wanted something to use at once and the smallest Corner House girl was eager to be helpful.

"I'll go! I'll go, Mrs. MacCall!" she cried, running for her hood and coat and overshoes, and, when she had donned them, seizing her Alice-doll, without which she seldom went anywhere, save to church and school. "I'll be there and back in just no time—you see if I'm not."

Mrs. MacCall told her carefully what she wanted, and gave her the dime.

"Oh, I'll 'member that!" Dot declared, with assurance, and she went out repeating it over and over to herself.

It was some distance to the druggist's and there were a lot of things to see on the way, and from frequent repetition of the name of the article the housekeeper wanted, the smallest Corner House girl arrived at her destination with only the sound and not much of the sense of it on her tongue.

"Good morning, little Miss Kenway," said the druggist, who knew Dot and her sisters very well. "What can I do for you?"

"Oh!" said Dot, breathlessly. "Mrs. MacCall wants a box of glory divine."

The druggist gasped, looked all around at his shelves helplessly, and murmured:

"What did you say it was you wanted?"

"Ten cents' worth of glory divine," repeated the smallest Corner House girl, positively.

"What—what does she do with it?" asked the druggist in desperation.

"Why—why, she puts it down the sink drain, and sprinkles it down cellar, an'—"

"Oh, my aunt!" groaned the druggist. "You mean chloride of lime?"

"Ye—yes, sir," admitted the somewhat abashed Dot. "I guess that's mebbe it."

Dot put the article purchased into the go-cart at Alice's feet, tucked the rug all around her cherished child, for it was a cold if sunny day, and started for home. As she wheeled the doll-carriage toward the Creamer cottage she saw the laundry wagon stop at that gate, while the driver jumped out and ran up the walk to the Creamers' side porch.

Dot knew that Mabel's mother always had her basket of soiled clothes ready for the man when he came and this occasion seemed to be no exception. There was the basket and the man grabbed it, ran back to the wagon, and, putting it in at the back, sprang up to his seat and rattled away to his next customer.

It was after Dot had returned to the old Corner House and delivered the box of "glory divine" to the housekeeper that the neighborhood was treated to a sensation originating in the Creamer cottage.

Tess had joined Dot in the yard of the old Corner House. The weather was much too cold for them to have all their dolls in the garden-house as they did in summer; but Neale had shoveled all the paths neatly since the last snow-storm, and the little girls could parade up and down with their doll carriages to their hearts' content.

They saw Mrs. Creamer run out upon her porch, look wildly around, and then she began to scream for Mabel.

"Mabel! Mabel! come here with the baby this moment! Didn't I tell you to let him sleep in the basket?"

Mabel appeared slowly from the back yard.

"You naughty child!" cried the worried woman. "You don't deserve to have a darling baby brother. And you broke his carriage, too—I verily believe—so you wouldn't have to wheel him in it. Where is he?"

"Ain't touched him," declared Mabel, sullenly.

"You—what do you mean? Where is the basket with the baby in it?" demanded Mrs. Creamer, wildly.

"Oh!" gasped Dot and—as she usually did when she was startled—she grabbed up her Alice-doll and hugged her to her bosom.

"I—I don't know," declared Mabel, looking rather scared now. "Honest, Mamma—I haven't seen him."

"He's been kidnapped! Thieves! Gypsies!"

The poor mother's shrieks might have been heard a block. Neighbors came running. Milton had only a small police force, but one of the officers chanced to be within hearing. He came, heard the exciting tale, and galloped off to the nearest telephone to let them know at headquarters that there was a child mysteriously missing.

"Why, isn't that funny?" said Dot to Tess. "If he was a kidnapper, he looked just like the laundryman."

"Who did?" demanded the amazed Theresa.

"The man who took the basket and stole Bubby Creamer."

"What ever are you saying, Dot Kenway?"

So Dot told her all that she had seen of the strange transaction.

"Why, that was the laundryman, of course!" declared Tess. "The baby is not stolen at all—at least he never meant to take it. I know the laundryman, and he's got seven children of his own. I don't believe he'd steal another."

The whole neighborhood was aroused. Agnes ran out into the yard to learn what the trouble was, and Tess and Dot, with great verbosity, related their version of the occurrence.

"Oh, children! we must tell Mrs. Creamer," Agnes said. "Of course the laundryman wouldn't have stolen the baby! He thought the basket held the wash and had been put out there for him."

She ran across the yard and swarmed over the fence into the Creamers' premises like a boy. Flying up to the group of lamenting women on the porch, she exploded her information among them like a bomb.

"Telephone to the laundry and find out if the man has got there yet," suggested one woman.

But Agnes knew that Mrs. Creamer's was one of the first places at which the laundryman stopped. He did not get back to the laundry until near noon.

Suddenly an automobile coming up Main Street attracted the Corner House girl's attention. She recognized the driver of the car, and ran out into the street, calling to him to stop.

"Oh, Joe Eldred! Wait! Wait!"

Joe was a boy somewhat older than Neale O'Neil, but one of the latter's closest friends. He was driving his father's car, having obtained a license only the month before.

"Joe! Wait!" Agnes repeated, waving her mittened hand to him.

"Hullo! Whose old cat is dead?" was his reply.

"Oh, Joe! such a dreadful thing has happened," Agnes said breathlessly. "Bubby Creamer has gone off with Mr. Billy Quirk, the laundryman, and his mother's worried to death."

"Whew! that's some kid!" exclaimed Joe. "Didn't know he could walk yet."

"He can't, silly!" returned Agnes, exasperated. "Listen!" and she told the boy how the wonder had occurred. "You know, Mr. Billy Quirk drives away out High Street to collect laundry. Won't you drive out that way and see if he's got poor little Bubby in his wagon?"

"Sure!" cried Joe. "Hop in!"

"But—but I didn't think of going."

"Say! You don't suppose I'd take a live baby aboard this car all alone?" gasped Joe. "I—guess—not!"

"Oh, I'll go!" agreed Agnes, and immediately slipped into the seat beside him. "Do hurry—do! Mrs. Creamer is almost crazy."

Joe's engine had been running all the time, and in a minute they rounded the corner into High Street.

"Neale got back yet?" asked Joe, slipping the clutch into high speed.

"Oh—oh!" gasped Agnes, as the car shot forward with suddenly increased swiftness. "How—how did you know he had gone away?"

"Saw him off Christmas morning."

"Oh, Joe Eldred! did you know Neale was going?"

"Why, not till he went," admitted the boy. "I was running down to the railroad station to meet my married sister and her kids—they were coming over for Christmas dinner—and I saw Neale lugging his satchel and legging it for the station. That bag weighed a ton, so I took him in."

"Where did he say he was going?" Agnes asked eagerly.

"He didn't say. Don't you know?"

"If I did I wouldn't ask you," snapped Agnes. "Mean old thing!"

"Hul-lo!" ejaculated Joe. "Who's mean?"

"Not you, Joe," the girl said sweetly. "But that Neale O'Neil. He went off without saying a word to any of us."

"Close mouthed as an oyster, Neale is. But I asked him what was in the bag, and what d' you s'pose he said?"

"I don't know," returned the girl, idly.

"He said: 'Either a hundred thousand dollars or nothing.' Now! what do you know about that?" demanded Joe, chuckling.

"What!" gasped Agnes, sitting straight up and staring at her companion.

"I guess if he'd been lugging such a fortune around it would have been heavy," added Joe, with laughter.

Agnes was silenced. For once the impulsive Corner House girl was circumspect. Neale's answer to Joe could mean but one thing. Neale must have carried away with him the old album she had found in the garret of the Corner House.

"Goodness gracious!" thought Agnes, feeling a queer faintness within. "It can't be that Neale O'Neil really believes that money and the bonds are good! That is too ridiculous! But, if not, what has he carried the book away with him for?

"He was going to show the bonds to somebody, he said. He went off in too great a hurry to do that. And did he take the book because the contents might be valuable and he was afraid to leave it behind him?"

"I never did hear of such a funny mix-up," concluded Agnes, still in her own mind. "And Ruth acts so strangely about it, too. She looked at the book first. Can it be possible that she thinks that old play money is real? Suppose some of it is good—just some of it?"

Agnes had begun to worry herself now about the old album and its contents. The mystery of it quite overshadowed in her mind the matter of the missing baby.

CHAPTER XII—MISS PEPPERILL'S DISASTER

The baby came first, after all, for Joe Eldred almost immediately exclaimed:

"Say, Aggie! isn't that Billy Quirk's wagon right ahead?"

"Oh, yes! Oh, yes, Joe!" Agnes agreed. "He hasn't got so far, after all."

"Do you believe he's got the kid?" demanded Joe, in doubt. "Look here! The back of the wagon's full of clothes baskets. Why! if the kid's there, he's buried!"

"Oh, don't!" cried Agnes. "Don't say such a thing, Joe!"

The boy had slowed down while speaking, and instantly Agnes was out of the car and had run ahead.

"Mr. Quirk! Oh, Mr. Quirk! Billy!" she shouted. "You've got a baby there!"

"Heh?" gasped the laundryman, who had been about to clamber into his seat again. "Got a baby!" he repeated, in a dazed sort of way, and actually turning pale. "Not another?"

"In your wagon, I mean. It's Mrs. Creamer's Bubby. Oh, dear, Mr. Quirk! do look quick and see if you've smothered him."

"What do you mean, girl? That I've smothered a baby!" groaned Mr. Quirk, who was a little, nervous man who could not stand much excitement.

"I don't know. Do look," begged Agnes. "Bubby was in the basket—not the soiled clothes—"

"Which basket?" cried the laundryman.

"The one you took away from the Creamers' porch, Billy," put in Joe Eldred, who had left the car, too. "Come on and look. Maybe the kid's all right."

"Oh, dear me! I hope so!" groaned Agnes. "What would Mrs. Creamer do—"

Joe helped the shaking laundryman to lift down the baskets of wash that were already stacked three tiers deep in the wagon.

"That's it! That's the one!" cried Agnes eagerly, recognizing Mrs. Creamer's basket.

And there was the baby, under a veil, sleeping as peacefully as could be. Fortunately the basket placed on top of the baby's temporary cradle had been the larger of the two, and had completely and safely covered the lower basket.

They got the baby, basket and all, into the back of the Eldred car without awakening Bubby, and Agnes sat beside him.

"I'll drive back as if I had a load of eggs," Joe declared, grinning. "If that kid wakes up and bawls, Aggie, what'll you do?"

"Humph!" said Agnes, with scorn, "isn't that just like a boy? Don't you suppose I know how to take care of a baby?"

Bubby did not awake, however, and their return to the Creamer cottage was like a triumphal entry. The neighborhood had turned out in a body. Mrs. Creamer ran a block up the street to meet the automobile, and she could not thank the Corner House girl and Joe Eldred enough.

But it was told of Mabel Creamer that she stood on the porch and scowled when they brought Bubby back in the basket. She actually did say to Tess and Dot, over the side fence:

"An' they blame me for it. Said I ought to have been there to watch what Billy Quirk was goin' to do. If it had been a really, truly Gypsy that had kidnapped Bubby, I s'pose they'd shut me up in jail!"

In a few days the little girls were back in school again, and Mabel was not obliged to stay in to mind the baby—hated task!—for she was in Dot's grade.

Tess' class gathered, too, to welcome Miss Pepperill's return to her wonted place—all but Sammy Pinkney. Sammy was a very sick boy and they brought straw and put it knee deep in Willow Street, in front of the Pinkney house, so as to deaden the sound of wagon wheels. Tess actually went on tiptoe when she passed the house where her schoolmate lay so ill.

Billy Bumps, the goat, that had once been Sammy's, looked longingly through the Corner House fence at the straw thus laid down, as though it was more tempting fodder than that with which Uncle Rufus supplied him.

"I believe Billy Bumps must know Sammy is awful sick," Tess said, in a hushed voice to Dot. "See how solemn he looks."

"Seems to me, Tess," Dot replied, "I never saw Billy Bumps look any other way. Why, he looked solemn when he eat-ed up Mrs. MacCall's stocking. I believe he must have a melancholic disposition."

"'Melancholic'! Goodness me, Dot!" snapped Tess, "I wish you wouldn't try to use words that you can't use."

"Why can't I use 'em, if I want to!" demanded Dot, stubbornly.

"But you get them all wrong."

"I guess I can use 'em if I want to—so now, Tess Kenway!" exclaimed Dot, pouting. "Words don't belong to anybody in particular, and I've as good a right to 'em as you have."

This revolt against her criticism rather staggered Tess. But she had much more serious problems to wrestle with at school just then.

In the first place Miss Pepperill was very "trying." Tess would not admit that the red-haired teacher was cross.

After a vacation of nearly two weeks the pupils had, of course, gotten quite out of hand. They were not only uneasy and had forgotten the school rules, but they seemed to Miss Pepperill to be particularly dull. Every little thing annoyed the teacher. She almost lost her voice trying to explain to the class the differences in tense—for they took up some simple grammar lessons in that grade.

One day Miss Pepperill completely lost her temper with Jakey Gerlach, who, in truth, was not her brightest pupil.

"I declare, Jakey, you never will get anywhere in school. You're always at the bottom of the class," she told him, sharply.

"Vell, does idt matter, teacher?" propounded Jakey, "whether I am at top or at bottom of de class? You teach de same at bot' ends."

At the end of each day the teacher was despairing. Tess always waited, timidly, to walk to the car with her. There was a crosstown car that made the trip from school to boarding house fairly easy for Miss Pepperill.

Perhaps, had she remained at the hospital with her sister, where she would have been more or less under Dr. Forsyth's eye, the final disaster in Miss Pepperill's case would not have arrived.

She really lost control of her scholars after a few days. In her room, where had always been the greatest decorum because the children feared her, there was now at times much confusion.

"Oh, children!" she gasped, holding her head in both hands, "I can't hear myself think!"

She sat down, unable to bear the hubbub of class recitation, and put her hands over her ears for a moment. Her eyes closed. The throbbing veins at her temples seemed about to burst.

It was Sadie Goronofsky who brought about the final catastrophe—and that quite innocently. Being unable at this juncture to attract attention by the usual means of waving her hand in the air and snapping her fingers, Sadie jumped up and went forward to Miss Pepperill's desk.

She had just sent away a class, and their clumsy footsteps had but ceased thundering on her eardrums when Sadie came on tiptoe to the platform. Miss Pepperill did not see her, but Sadie, tired of weaving her arm back and forth without result, clutched the edge of the light shawl Miss Pepperill wore over her shoulders.

The jerk the child gave the shawl was sufficient to pull Miss Pepperill's elbow from the edge of the desk where it rested, her hand upholding her throbbing head.

In her weakness the teacher almost pitched out of her chair to the floor. She shrieked.

Sadie Goronofsky flew back to her seat in terror. Miss Pepperill opened her eyes and saw nobody near. It was just as though an invisible hand had pulled at the shawl and had dislodged her elbow.

She was not of a superstitious nature, but her nerves were unstrung. She uttered another shriek—then a third.

The children under her care were instantly alarmed. They rose and ran from her, or cowered, whimpering, in their seats, while the poor hysterical woman uttered shriek after shriek.

Her cries brought other teachers into the room. They found her with her hair disarranged, her dress disheveled, beating her heels on the platform and shrieking at the top of her voice—quite out of her mind for the time being.

The children were dismissed at once and took to their homes excited and garbled reports of the occurrence.

Tess did not go home at once. She saw them finally take Miss Pepperill, now exhausted and moaning, out to a taxi-cab and drive away with her to the Women's and Children's Hospital, where Mrs. Eland was.

But the damage was done. Poor Miss Pepperill's mind was, for the time, quite out of her control. The next day she had to be removed to the state hospital for the insane because she disturbed the other patients under her sister's care.

That ended, of course, Miss Pepperill's career as a public school teacher. With a record of having been at the insane hospital, she could hope never again to preside over a class of children in the public school. Her occupation and manner of livelihood were taken from her.

"It is a terrible, terrible thing," Ruth said at dinner, the day Miss Pepperill was taken to the state hospital.

Ruth had been with Tess to call on Mrs. Eland, and the little gray lady had told them all about it.

"I am awfully sorry for my Mrs. Eland, too," Tess said. "I am sure she could have cared for Miss Pepperill if they'd let her stay."

"Don't worry, honey," Agnes said quickly. "They'll soon let Miss Pepperill come back."

"But the harm is done," Ruth rejoined gravely. "Just as Dr. Forsyth said, she ought to take a long, long rest."

"If they were only rich," sighed Agnes.

"If we were only rich!" Ruth rejoined.

"My goodness! and wouldn't we be rich—just!—if all that stage money I found was only real, Ruthie?" Agnes whispered to her elder sister.

Ruth grew very red and said, quite tartly for her: "I don't see that it would do us any good—if it were so. You let it go out of your hands very easily."

"Oh, pshaw! Neale will bring it back," said Agnes, half laughing, yet wondering that Ruth should be so earnest. "You speak just as though you believed it was good money."

"You don't know, one way or another, whether it is so or not."

"Why, Ruth!"

"Well, you don't, do you?" demanded the elder sister.

"How silly you talk. You're as bad as Neale about those old bonds. I believe he lugged that book off with him just to show somebody the bonds to see if they were any good."

Ruth turned away, and said nothing more regarding the album; but Agnes was more and more puzzled about the whole affair. The two girls were not confiding in each other. Nothing, of course, could have shaken Agnes' belief in Neale's honesty. While, on the other hand, Ruth feared that the ex-circus-boy had fallen before temptation.

Believing, as she did, that the banknotes found in the album were all good, the oldest Corner House girl considered that the bonds might be of great value, too. Altogether, as Neale had figured up, there was over a hundred thousand dollars in the album.

This fortune was somewhere—so Ruth believed—in the possession of a thoughtless, if not really dishonest, boy. A thousand things might happen to the treasure trove Neale O'Neil had borne away from the old Corner House.

No matter whether it were Neale himself or another who made wrong use of the money or the bonds, if they were lost it would be a catastrophe. Neither the Corner House girls, nor whoever properly owned the book, would ever be benefitted by the odd find in the garret of the Stower homestead.

Who the actual owner—or owners—of the treasure was, Ruth could not imagine. But that she was the proper custodian of the album until Mr. Howbridge returned, the girl was quite sure.

She dared take nobody into her confidence until their guardian came home. Least of all could she talk about it to Agnes. And on her part, Agnes was quite as loath to speak of the matter, in earnest, to Ruth.

What Joe Eldred had said about Neale and his heavy satchel really alarmed Agnes. A hundred thousand dollars! A fortune, indeed.

"Goodness me!" Agnes thought. "Neale is never silly enough to believe that the money is real, is he? Impossible! Yet—why did he carry the old thing off with him?

"It bothers Ruth—I can see that. I don't know what idea she's got in her head; but surely both of them can't be mad about that money and those bonds. Goodness! am I the only sensible one in the family?" the flyaway asked herself, quite seriously.

"For I know very well that stuff in the old album is nothing but 'green goods.' Maybe somebody, years ago, used it dishonestly—used it to fool other people. And suppose Neale is fooling himself with it?"

For it never entered the loyal Agnes' mind that her boy chum was other than the soul of honesty.

CHAPTER XIII—AGNES IN THE WOODS

Perfectly dreadful things were always happening to Dot Kenway's Alice-doll. That child certainly was born under an unlucky star, as Mrs. MacCall often declared.

Yet she was the most cherished of all the smallest Corner House girl's large and growing family of doll-babies. Dot lived with the Alice-doll in a world of make-believe, and where romance lapped over the border of reality it was hard for Dot to tell.

The children—Dot and Tess—fed the birds from the bedroom windows whenever the snow was on the ground. And Neale, when he was at hand, hung pieces of fat and suet in the trees for the jays and shrikes, and other of the "meat-eaters."

The smaller birds were so tame that they hopped right upon the window-sills to eat. On one sill Neale had built a rather ingeniously contrived "sleeping porch" for the Alice-doll, in which Dot put her—bundled in Uncle Rufus' napkin-bag—every night. The screened side served as a ventilator for the children's bedroom.

The top of this boxlike arrangement was of oiled paper, pasted over a wooden frame, and one eager sparrow, pecking at crumbs on the taut paper, burst a hole right through; so he, or another, hopped saucily down through the hole and tried to peck out the Alice-doll's bead-like eyes!

"Why—why—you cannibal!" gasped Dot, and ran to her child's rescue.

With a frightened chirp the sparrow shot up through the torn paper and winged his flight over the housetop.

"You'll have to paste up that hole, Dot," Tess said, "or something more than a sparrow will get in at your Alice-doll."

"Oh, me! what shall I do?" moaned Dot. "Alice must sleep in her porch. The doctors all say so."

"I've a piece of silk you may have to paste over the top of your porch, honey," Ruth said. "That will let the light through, and the birds won't peck it to shreds."

"Oh, thank you, sister!" said Dot, much relieved.

"I'll run for the glue bottle," Tess added, wishing to be helpful.

But having brought the bottle Tess was obliged to help Agnes with the beds. There were certain duties the Corner House girls had to do every day, and on Saturdays three of the early morning hours at least were spent by all of them save Dot in housework of one kind or another, and even she had some light household duties. The house was very large and Mrs. MacCall and Linda could not do all the work. As for Aunt Sarah Maltby, she only "ridded up" her own room, and never lifted her fingers to work outside it.

So just now Dot was left alone with the silk and the glue bottle. It was not a difficult task, and even Dot might be expected to do it with neatness and despatch.

But when Ruth chanced to come into the room some time later, Dot was still struggling with the glue bottle. She had not yet been successful in removing the cork.

"Goodness me! what a mean, mean thing," Dot cried, quite unaware that she was being observed. "Now I tell you what," she added, addressing the cork with which she was struggling, "I'm going to get you out, if I have to push you in—so there!"

This cheered up the family considerably when it was repeated; but Dot was used to furnishing amusement for the Corner House family. Usually the hour spent at the dinner table was the most enjoyable of all the day for the girls, for all that had happened during the day was there and then discussed.

It had been just the evening before that Dot was taken to task quite seriously by Ruth for a piece of impoliteness of which the little girl stood confessed.

"Sister was sorry to see this afternoon, when you were talking at the gate with Mr. Seneca Sprague, Dot, that you ate cookies out of a paper bag and did not offer Mr. Sprague any."

"Didn't," said Dot. "'Twas crackers."

"Well, crackers, then. You should always offer any person whom you are with, a share of your goodies."

"Why, Ruthie!" exclaimed Dot. "You know very well Seneca Sprague wouldn't have eaten any of those crackers."

"Why not?" asked Ruth, still serious.

"Isn't he a—a vegetablearian?" propounded Dot, quite warmly.

"A vegetarian—yes," admitted the older sister.

"Well!" exclaimed Dot, in triumph, "he wouldn't have eaten 'em then. They were animal crackers."

Agnes made her preparations that evening for a visit she proposed to make the next day. After their work was done on Saturday the Corner House girls sometimes separated to follow different paths for the remainder of the holiday. This week Agnes was going to visit Mr. Bob Buckham and his invalid wife, who lived some distance from Milton, but not far off the interurban car line.

When she started about ten o'clock to go to the car, not only Tess and Dot, but Tom Jonah was ready to accompany her. The old dog was always glad to be in any expedition; but Agnes did not want him to follow the car and she told him to go back.

"Oh, don't do that, sister," begged Tess. "We'll look out for Tom Jonah. You know he'll mind us—Dot and me. We'll bring him home from the corner."

So he was allowed to pace sedately behind the trio to the corner of Ralph Avenue where Agnes purposed to take the car. This was not far down Main Street from the Parade Ground, and the children could easily find their way home again.

As the three sisters passed the drug store they saw coming out a woman in long, black garments, a veil, and a huge collar and a sort of hood of starched white linen.

Dot's eyes grew big and round as she watched this figure, and finally she whispered: "Oh, Aggie; who is that?"

"That is a sister of charity," replied Agnes.

Dot pondered deeply for a moment and then returned to the charge with: "Say, Aggie, which sister is she—Faith or Hope?"

"Hear that child!" sighed Tess. "I never heard of such a ridiculous question, did you, Aggie?" she asked the laughing, older sister.

Just then the car Agnes must take came along and the older girl ran to climb aboard, after kissing the little ones good-bye. And there was Tom Jonah, bounding right behind her.

"No, no! You must not! You can't, Tom Jonah," Agnes cried, stopping at the car step. "Go back, Tom Jonah!"

The dog's ears and tail drooped. He turned slowly away, disappointed.

"You know I can't take you in the car," Agnes said. "Go home with Tess and Dottie."

She stepped aboard. The conductor just then rang the bell for starting. Agnes pitched into a seat as the car jumped forward and failed to see whether the dog returned to her sisters or not.

It was a long ride in rather a round-about way to the Buckham farm. Mr. Bob Buckham raised strawberries for market and was a good friend of the Corner House girls. Agnes particularly was a favorite of the farmer and his invalid wife.

Although the interurban car passed one end of the Buckham farm, there was another point where Agnes could leave the car to cut across lots and through the woods to reach the house. She had been this way once with Neale, and she thought it a much pleasanter, if somewhat longer, walk.

So, when the car came to the road in the woods which the Corner House girl was sure was the right one, she signaled the conductor to stop and she stepped down into the snow beside the track.

Agnes was to learn, however, that the woods look different under a blanket of snow, from what they do when the ground is bare.

The road into which she ventured was merely a track leading into a place where cordwood had been cut. Wagons had gone back and forth, but not for several days. The path led in a direction quite different from the Buckham house and every minute she walked this way took her farther and farther from the road to Strawberry Farm.

The air was invigorating, the sun shone, and the path was hard under her feet, so Agnes found the walk very pleasant indeed. Being quite unconscious of her mistake, nothing troubled her mind. She tramped on, rejoicing, expecting to come into familiar territory within a mile or so.

The forest grew thicker as she advanced. The only tracks she saw in the snow on either side of the wood road were those of birds and rabbits. Jays shot through the leafless woods shouting their raucous call; crows cawed in the distance; close at hand, squirrels chattered and scolded at her from the trees as she passed under the stark, bare branches.

Finally the impression was forced upon Agnes Kenway's mind that the wood was very lonely. She heard no axe—and an axe can be heard for miles. She noticed, too, at length, that the tracks in the road—both of men and horses—were not fresh. She had not observed before that a light snow powdered these marks—and it had not snowed for three days.

"Why! can it be possible that nobody has been to Mr. Buckham's by this road for so long?" murmured Agnes.

She turned around to look behind her. As she did so some creature—quite a big and shaggy animal—darted across the path and disappeared in the brush.

Mercy! How startled Agnes was for a moment. It might be a bear! Or a wolf! Then, of course, she came to herself, shrugged her shoulders, and laughed.

"It's a dog. Somebody is out hunting. But goodness! how he did scare me," she thought.

Agnes went on again, cheerfully enough. The road was by no means straight. If she looked back she could see only a short distance, for the brush and trees hid the back stretches.

She turned again. There was the creature just darting once more into the shrubbery!

Agnes halted in her tracks. She was suddenly smitten with fear. She could not shake the feeling off. Surely there was something dogging her footsteps.

She puckered her lips to whistle; but no sound came. She tried to call; but her tongue seemed dry and her throat contracted. She knew it was a dog; yet the possibility of its being some savage beast instead, terrified her.

Even a bad dog would be dangerous to meet in this lonely place. And he followed her so stealthily!

Agnes was panic-stricken at midday. It was almost noon now, and how strange that she had not reached the Buckham house! Why! she had been walking for an hour.

It came over the girl suddenly that she was lost.

"Yet I don't see how that can be," she murmured. "I'm in the road and it's plain enough. Surely it should lead somewhere."

Nevertheless she would have turned about and gone back to the car tracks had it not been for the apparition that seemed dogging her steps.

She dared not turn back and face that Unknown!

Slily she looked over her shoulder again. There it was—dim, shaggy, slinking close to the snow. Agnes was sure now that she knew what it was. Naught but a wolf would act like that—would trail her so silently and with such determination.

Agnes was truly terror-stricken. She began to run—and running was not easy in this rutty road. She fell once; but she did not mind the bruises and scratches she received, for all she could think of was that the wolf might leap upon her while she was down.

Up the poor girl scrambled and ran on, crying now—all her brave temper quenched. She dared look behind no more. How close her awful pursuer was she dared not know.

On and on she hastened; now running, now walking fast, her limbs shaking with dread and weariness. It seemed as though she must come to some habitation soon. She had had no idea that there was any such wilderness as this anywhere back of Milton!

There were no signs here of man's nearness save the road through the forest, nor had she seen such since leaving the main highway. As she said, surely this road must lead somewhere.

Suddenly Agnes smelled smoke. She saw it rising between the trees ahead. Escape from the prowling beast was at hand. The girl hurried on. The place where the smoke was rising was down a little slope, at the foot of which she suddenly discovered the railroad. She knew something about the locality then. It was some distance from Mr. Bob Buckham's house.

This was a lonely place, too. There was no station anywhere near. Heaps of ties lay about—cords and cords of them. It suddenly smote upon the girl's mind that tramps might be here. Tramps followed the railroad line. And tramps might be more to be feared than a wolf!

She halted in her tracks and waited to get her breath. Of course she glanced fearfully behind again. But the prowling beast was no longer in sight. The vicinity of the fire had doubtless made him hesitate and draw off.

So Agnes could take her time about approaching the campfire. She was sure that was what it must be. The smoke arose from beyond a great heap of railroad ties, and now, when her pulses stopped beating so in her ears, she distinguished voices.

Well! human beings were at hand. She could not help feeling suspicious of them; yet their nearness had driven off the strange and terrible beast that had so frightened her.

After a minute or two the Corner House girl crept forward. Some of her usual courage returned to her. Her heart beat high and her color rose. She bit her lower lip with her pretty, even teeth, as she always did when she labored under suppressed excitement, and tiptoed to the end of the piled up ties.

The voices were louder here—more easily distinguished. There were two of them—a young voice and an old voice. And in a moment she discovered something that pleased and relieved her. The young voice was a girl's voice— Agnes was quite positive of that.

She thought at once: "No harm can come to me if there is a girl here. But who can she be, camping out in the snowy woods?"

In another moment she would have stepped around the corner of the pile of ties and revealed herself to the strangers had not something that was said reached her ears—and that something was bound to arrest Agnes Kenway's attention.

"A book full of money."

The young voice said this, and then the other spoke, it seemed, doubtingly.

Again came the girl's voice with passionate earnestness:

"I tell you I saw it! I know 'twas money."

"It don't sound reasonable," and the man's husky voice was plainer now.

"I tell you I saw it. I had the book in my hand."

"Why didn't you bring it away and let me see it?" demanded the other.

"I'd ha' done it, Pop, if I'd been let. He had it in his bag in his room. I got in and had the book in my hand. It's heavy and big, I tell you! He came in and caught me messin' with his things, and I thought he'd lam me! You know, Neale always was high tempered," added the strange young voice.

Agnes was powerless to move. Mention of money in a book was sufficient to hold her in her tracks. But now they were speaking of Neale O'Neil!

"Where'd he ever get so much money?" demanded the husky voice.

"Stole it, mebbe."

"None of the Sorbers was ever light-fingered—you've got to say that much for them."

"What's that boy doing with all that money, and we so poor?" snarled the young voice, "Wasn't you hurt when that gasoline tank exploded in the big top, just the same as Bill Sorber? And nobody made any fuss over you."

"Well, well, well," muttered the man.

"They're not carin' what becomes of us—neither Twomley nor Sorber. Here you've been laid up, and it's mid-winter and too late for us to get any job till the tent shows open in the spring. An' we must beat it South like hoboes. I say 'tisn't fair!" and the young voice was desperate.

"There ain't many things fair in this world, Barnabetta," said the husky voice, despondently.

"I—I'd steal that money from Neale Sorber if I got the chance. And he'll be coming back to this very next town with it. That's where he's living now—at Milton. I hate all the Sorbers." "There, there, Barnabetta! Don't take on so.

We'd have got into some good act in vaudeville 'fore now if I hadn't had to favor my ankle."

"You'd better've let me go into that show alone, Pop."

"No, no, my girl. You're too young for that. No, that warn't the right kind of a show."

The girl's voice sounded wistful now: "Wish we could get an act like that we had in the tent show when Neale was with us. He was a good kid then."

"Yes; but there ain't many like Neale Sorber was. And like enough he's gone stale 'fore now."

"I'd just like to know where he got all that money," said the girl-voice. "And in a book, too. I thought 'twas a photograph album."

"Hist!" said the man-voice, "'Tisn't so much where he got it as it is, is he comin' back here with it."

"He'll come back to Milton, sure. Bill Sorber isn't so sick now."

The voices died to a whisper. Agnes, both troubled and frightened, tried to steal away. But she had been resting her weight upon the corner of the heap of ties. As she moved, the icy timbers shook, slid, and suddenly overturned.

Agnes, her face white, and with a terrified air, found herself facing a man and, not a girl but, a boy, who had sprung up from a log by the fire. And they knew she had overheard their conversation.

CHAPTER XIV—BARNABETTA

"Why, there isn't any girl here at all!" Agnes Kenway exclaimed, as she faced the two people who had been sitting by the bonfire.

They were shabby people and both had bundles tied to the end of stout staves. Evidently they had either walked far, or had stolen a ride upon a freight train to this spot. There was a water-tank in sight.

The boy, who was thin, and tall, and wiry looking, slipped the bundle off his stick, and seizing the stick itself as a club, advanced stealthily around one side of the fire. The man seemed to be a much more indecisive sort of creature. His smooth face was like parchment; his ears stood out like bats' wings. No one could honestly call him good looking. Rather was he weak looking; and his expression was one of melancholy.

Somehow, Agnes was not much afraid of the man. It was the boy who made her tremble. He looked so wild, and his eyes blazed so as he clutched the stick, creeping nearer to Agnes all the time.

As he advanced, Agnes began to retreat, stepping slowly backward. She would have run at once, trusting to her lightness of foot to relieve her of the boy's company in a few rods, had it not been that she remembered the unknown and savage beast that had followed her to this spot.

It must have been this boy's voice she had heard; yet it sounded just like a girl's. Agnes was greatly puzzled by the youth's appearance. She looked again over his supple, crouching body as he advanced. It was wide-hipped, narrow-waisted, and not at all boyish looking. Despite the thinness of this young stroller, his figure did not at all suggest the angles of a boy's frame.

Aside from being puzzled, Agnes Kenway was much afraid of him. His face was so keenly threatening in expression, and his stealthy actions so antagonistic, that the Corner House girl almost screamed aloud. Finally, she found relief in speech.

"What are you going to do with that stick? Put it down!" she cried.

"I—I——You've been listening to us talking," said the boy. But it was the girl's voice that spoke.

It did not sound like a boy's voice at all. It was too high, and there was a certain sweetness to it despite the tremor of the notes. Agnes began to recover her self-possession. She might have been afraid of a reckless boy. But she was strong herself, and agile. Even if the other did have a stick—

"You were listening," cried the other accusingly, again. "Yes, I was listening—a little," confessed the Corner House girl. "But so would you—"

"No, I wouldn't. That's sneaky," snapped the other.

"How about your finding out about the book of money you spoke of?" asked Agnes, boldly. "Didn't you do anything 'sneaky' to find out aboutthat?"

The other started and dropped the stick. The man sat down suddenly. It was plain, even to usually unobservant Agnes Kenway, that her remark had startled both of them.

"I was alone—and lost," Agnes went on to explain. "I was trying to reach Mr. Bob Buckham's farm, and a wolf chased me—"

"A wolf!" interrupted the youthful tramp. "Now I know you're telling a wicked story."

"It was. Or something," said Agnes, stoutly. "I was scared. Then I saw your smoke."

"Why didn't you walk right in and speak to us instead of snoopin'?"

"You'd have 'snooped'," flashed back Agnes, with some heat. "I was alone, and I was afraid of tramps—"

"Well, we're tramps," said the boy, stooping and picking up the dropped stick.

"Not the kind I am afraid of," Agnes replied, trying to smile.

The boy would not be pacified, but the man said, shakingly, from his seat on the log:

"We wouldn't hurt you, girl. Put down that stick, Barney. This is my son, Barney, and I'm Asa Scruggs. I'm a joey when I'm in luck, and Barney—he's a trapeze artist. He's good."

"Oh, Pop!" shrilled the youthful trapeze artist, "might's well tell the truth this time. She's nothing but a girl herself."

"And that's what you are!" cried Agnes, with excitement.

"Yes. I'm Barnabetta, not Barney, Scruggs. Nice name, isn't it?" scoffed the strange girl. "My mother was Pennsylvania Dutch; that's where I got my name, Barnabetta. But it's safer to travel as a boy, so I'm Barney on the road. Besides, skirts would be in the way, climbing in and out of 'rattlers.'"

"Oh, what fun!" gasped Agnes. "Do you and your father always travel this way?"

"You bet we don't! Not when we have an engagement. We've ridden in Pullman cars—haven't we, Pop?"

The man nodded. He did not say much but watched Agnes with eyes that, in a child, the girl would have thought expressed terror. Barnabetta was much the stronger character of the two, the Corner House girl was positive.

"But where are you traveling now?" asked the interested Agnes.

"We're aimin' on gettin' South, miss. There's tent shows there all winter long," said the man, plaintively. "I've been laid up with my ankle, and it's too late to get any bookings worth while through the usual vaudeville agencies. We been workin' for Twomley & Sorber's Herculean Circus and Menagerie; but of course they're in winter quarters now at Tiverton. That's where I got hurt—right at the end of the season, too."

Agnes' brain was working busily. Twomley & Sorber's at Tiverton. Tiverton was where the letter was postmarked that had taken Neale O'Neil away from home so strangely. The talk she had just overheard assured her that these two circus performers had been conversing about Neale and the old album full of money and bonds that he had taken away with him.

But she caught the disguised Barnabetta watching her very sharply. That girl's black eyes were like glittering steel points. They seemed to say: "How much does this girl who listened guess—how much does she suspect—how much does she know?"

"We've got to work up some kind of patter to go with our act if we strike a job," said Barnabetta, still with her eyes fixed on the Corner House girl. "You've got to have something new if you expect to put any act over these days. Pop's a good joey—"

"I suppose you mean a clown?" asked Agnes.

"Yep. How'd you know?" sharply retorted Barnabetta.

"I—I've heard the word used before," admitted Agnes, seeing that she had been unwise. "Then you know circus folks?" observed the suspicious trapeze artist.

"Oh, no!"

Barnabetta was not convinced, that was plain. But she turned in a matter-of-fact way to the man. "Well, Pop," she said coolly, "about that money." The man jumped, and his weak eyes opened wide. But Barnabetta kept right on and Agnes was sure she was winking at her father. "You must disbelieve me when I say I saw it, and I'm goin' to say we'll get it," she declared.

"Huh?" gasped the clown.

"That's the way it must be in our act," the girl said firmly. "In our act—don't you see?"

"Oh! Ha! Hum!" said the clown, clearing his throat. "I see."

"This is second-story work," the girl explained eagerly. "I'll show you how to climb up to the window for the money—that's to the trapeze, you see," she added, throwing the explanation at Agnes.

"Oh! I see," murmured the Corner House girl.

"And you play the joey part, Pop," pursued Barnabetta. "I'll go ahead, and say 'Hist!' and 'Take care!' and 'Clumsy!' and the like, making believe we're going to rob a house. You do the joey, as I said, and climb almost up to the trapeze on the rope, and then make a fall. We've got to get the laughs," she added again, glancing sidewise at Agnes.

The latter felt very peculiar indeed. Bluntly honest, it was hard for Agnes to play a part in this way. She knew the girl trapeze performer was trying to lead her astray. Barnabetta and her father were talking of Neale and his money before Agnes appeared, and this tale about the new act was being invented on the spur of the moment to confuse her.

Barnabetta stopped suddenly. Perhaps she saw that her tale was making little impression upon their visitor.

"Where were you going, miss?" asked Mr. Scruggs, after a minute's silence.

"I was on my way to visit Mr. and Mrs. Buckham. They expect me," said Agnes, wisely. "But I must have missed the road. I know where I am now, however, I'll go down the railroad beyond the water-tank a little way and find the very crossing of the lane that goes into their dooryard from the west. Those trees must hide the house from here."

Secretly Agnes wanted to get away, but not to visit Mr. and Mrs. Buckham. She felt that she ought to communicate with Neale O'Neil just as soon as possible. This old clown and his disguised daughter might have a plan to stop Neale on his way home and take the old album and its precious contents away from him.

For now Agnes, like her sister, Ruth, had begun to believe that the engraved slips of paper pasted into the book were "really truly" banknotes. How they had gotten there, and who they originally belonged to, Agnes could not guess. Nor did she believe that Neale O'Neil had carried them off with him, knowing them to be good currency.

However, everybody who got a sight of them seemed to think that the notes were legal tender. Even this strange girl, Barnabetta Scruggs, thought Neale was carrying around thousands of dollars with him. Dear me! if Neale would only know enough to go to Mr. Howbridge, there at his brother's house at Tiverton, the lawyer would tell him just what to do with the old album.

These thoughts raced like lightning through Agnes' mind as she turned calmly away from the campfire. "I must be going," she said. "Good-bye."

The man said nothing, but looked away. Barnabetta said: "How about that wolf you said was chasing you?" and she said it sneeringly, as though she doubted Agnes' story.

"I guess he won't follow me down upon the railroad tracks," the Corner House girl said cheerfully.

"Huh! I guess he won't. 'Cause why? There wasn't any wolf," snapped Barnabetta. "That's a story!"

"It isn't, either!" cried Agnes, hotly.

"I'd like to know what you were hidin' behind that pile of ties and listenin' to us for?" said the circus girl.

"I told you how I came to do that."

"I don't believe you," was the flat reply.

Agnes was too impulsive to let this stand without answering. She whirled and spoke hotly to the trapeze performer:

"I tell you the truth. I doubt if you tell me the truth. Why were you so afraid of being overheard, if all that talk about the money you saw in the book was just play-acting?"

"You are too smart," snarled Barnabetta.

"I am smart enough to know that you are trying to fool me. I'm not going to believe you at all—not a word you say. I don't like you. I'm going to Mr. Buckham's—so now!"

Barnabetta sprang forward, crying: "You're not goin' so fast! Is she, Pop?"

Agnes had forgotten the clown. He had come silently around the other side of the fire—evidently at some signal from Barnabetta—and was now right at her elbow.

"Grab her, Pop! Don't let her get away!" cried the circus girl, commandingly.

Agnes would have run; but she fairly bumped into the little man. He seized her by both arms, and she found that she was powerless against him.

At this point Agnes Kenway became thoroughly frightened. She opened her lips and screamed for help.

Instantly there was a scrambling in the brush beside the overturned pile of ties, a savage growl, and a shaggy body sprang into sight and charged the struggling Corner House girl and the man who held her.

CHAPTER XV—AGNES SHOULDERS RESPONSIBILITY

"Tom Jonah!" screamed Agnes; for in this emergency she recognized the old dog.

He had followed the car from town, had scented out her tracks when she entered the woods, and so had followed Agnes to this spot, afraid to come up with her for fear of being scolded; for, of course, he knew well enough he had disobeyed.

But now the dog's loyalty to one of his little mistresses had brought Tom Jonah out of hiding. The attempt of Asa Scruggs to hold Agnes was an unfortunate move on the clown's part.

Tom Jonah shot out of the bushes, growling fiercely, and charged the man. Scruggs let go of Agnes and shrank back, trying to flee—for the dog looked quite as savage as the wolf Agnes had thought was following her.

As he turned, Scruggs slipped and went down. His right foot twisted under him and the dog's heavy body flung him flat on his back. Tom Jonah held the clown down with both forepaws on his chest and a threatening muzzle at his throat.

Agnes could easily have gotten away now. The clown could not move, and Barnabetta began to cry.

"Oh, Pop! Oh, Pop!" she wailed. "He's going to eat you up!"

Agnes knew Tom Jonah would not let the man rise unless she commanded him to do so. So she did not leave the spot as she had at first intended. All in an instant, through the interference of the old dog, the tables had been turned.

"If I call him off," she asked, shakingly, of Barnabetta, "will you leave me alone?"

"You've fixed Pop with your nasty old dog—hasn't she, Pop? That's his bad ankle. He can't do anything to you now," declared the trapeze performer.

"And you let that stick alone," commanded Agnes. "Tom Jonah will do anything I tell him to," she added, warningly, and then proved it by calling the old dog to come to her. He came, growling, and showing the red of his eyes as he looked over his shoulder at the prostrate clown. The man seemed unable to rise, but sat up, groaning, and rubbing the twisted ankle.

"Oh, dear, me!" cried Barnabetta; "that fixes us for another two months. You won't be able to work at all, Pop, even if we get a job. What ever shall we do?"

Agnes began to feel most unhappy. Her excitement once past, she felt that she was somehow partly to blame for the clown's predicament. And she could not help feeling sorry for him and for this strange girl who was dressed in boy's apparel.

Besides, Agnes felt a sort of admiration for Barnabetta Scruggs. There was romance attached to her. A girl, not much older than Agnes herself, tramping in boy's clothing and meeting all sorts of adventures on the road! Agnes failed to remember that right then Barnabetta and her father were meeting with one very unpleasant adventure.

"Dear me," said the Corner House girl, with sympathy. "Is he really hurt?"

"That's his sprained ankle hurt again. It's even worse than just an ordinary sprain," explained the trapeze performer. "He can't do any stunts, or joey work on crutches, can he? The doctor told him to be careful for a long time with it. What shall we do?"

"He—he won't be able to walk, will he?" gasped Agnes.

"Only on a crutch. We can't do any travelin' on railroads with him this way. And he can't walk. How far's it to Milton?"

"You can get an electric car to town if you follow this woodpath."

"How far?"

"I've been almost an hour and a half walking here from the car."

"Must be four or five miles then," murmured Barnabetta.

"Yes."

"Never can hobble that far—can you, Pop?" asked the circus girl.

"Not yet," groaned the man. He was taking off his shoe and sock. "Get me some snow, Barnabetta," he said.

"My, that's so!" she exclaimed. "We can pack it in snow to take down the swellin'."

"He'll get his foot frostbitten sitting here without any shoe on," said Agnes.

"I'll keep a good fire goin'," said the girl, shortly.

"And stay here all night—in the open?" cried Agnes, horror-stricken at such a thought.

"Where else?" snapped Barnabetta. "There's no place to go. We've got no friends, anyway. And we've mighty little money. We expected to steal a ride South, and sleep in farmers' barns, and the like. We've done it before. But we've never been so bad off as this."

She said all this too low for her father to hear. She added: "Pop always had his health and strength before."

"Oh, dear me!" groaned Agnes, impulsively. "I wish Neale were here."

"Oh!" ejaculated the circus girl, sharply. "What Neale's that?"

Agnes remained silent, sorry that she had spoken so thoughtlessly.

"I might have known you were one of those girls," added Barnabetta.

"What girls?" asked Agnes, curiously.

"Those that Neale O'Neil lives with at Milton."

"He doesn't live with us. He lives next door to us—with Mr. Con Murphy."

"Bill Sorber said he lived with some Corner House girls. That's what he called you," said Barnabetta.

"Just the same," said Agnes, boldly; "I wish he were here. He'd know what to do—how to help you."

But Barnabetta was despondent. "Nobody can't help us," she said. "We're in bad."

"Oh! I will find some way of helping," declared Agnes, trying to speak comfortingly.

"Huh! lots of good you can do now," grumbled the other. "You and that nasty dog has just fixed Pop."

"It wasn't Tom Jonah's fault. And I'm sure it wasn't my fault. He was only defending me. You and your father shouldn't have tried to stop me."

"You hid the dog in the bushes a-purpose," cried Barnabetta, angrily. "You know you did."

"No, I didn't. And he scared me enough, too. I thought he was a wolf," said Agnes, anxious to explain though why she should be put on the defensive, it would be difficult to tell.

"Well," concluded Barnabetta, roughly, "you can't be any good here."

"I know I can't. But I believe I can help you just the same."

"Don't want your help," growled the circus girl.

"Oh! don't say that," begged the Corner House girl. "I can go to Mr. Bob Buckham and get his carriage and horses—"

"We haven't got any money to pay for a carriage," said Barnabetta, quickly.

"You won't have to pay Mr. Buckham for doing an act of Christian charity," declared Agnes, and she set off immediately, Tom Jonah following closely at her heels.

Barnabetta did not even bid her good-bye. She was all solicitude for her father's hurt ankle, and was now kneeling by him, packing the snow about the swelling foot. But she was "as hard as nails" toward the Corner House girl.

Agnes hurried right down to the railroad and walked without molestation to the crossing she had spoken of. There, up the snowy lane, she obtained her first glimpse of Mr. Bob Buckham's house.

She had come a roundabout way to it, indeed. It was now long past noon and she had missed her dinner. Of course, Mr. and Mrs. Buckham had ceased expecting her long ago.

The big girl who worked in Mrs. Buckham's kitchen—Posey by name and an autocrat to a degree—met Agnes with a cheerful greeting, but refused admission to Tom Jonah.

"No. He can't come in. I just been scrubbin' my floor and I can't 'low no dog trackin' it up. You drop your arctics there on the porch, Miss Aggie, and then you can run in to Mrs. Buckham."

"If Tom Jonah only wore arctics!" sighed the Corner House girl.

"Well, he don't—more's the pity," agreed Posey.

Agnes ran into the invalid's room, all breathless, but full of her adventure. There sat Mrs. Buckham in her wheel-chair, surrounded by bright worsteds and fancywork, as busy and smiling as though she had not spent twenty years between that chair and her bed.

"Here's our Corner House girl at last. And why not to dinner?" cried Mrs. Buckham.

"Oh, mercy me! I didn't even re-mem-ber dinner till just this minute!" Agnes confessed.

"Your poor child! No dinner? Quick, Posey! here's a starving child—"

"Dear Mrs. Buckham—wait! Never mind me. I sha'n't starve yet," declared the plump Agnes, laughing. "Look at me. Do I seem so frail? And I've had the greatest adventure!"

"Well, well!"

"Where is Mr. Buckham? I must tell him all about it, too," Agnes said, excitedly.

And here came the farmer as she spoke—bewhiskered, grizzled, keen-eyed and always smiling, who cried:

"Here's the tardy one! Why, I thought you were coming out betimes, young lady? How are all at the Corner House?"

Agnes was too greatly excited to reply in full to that question. Mr. Bob Buckham sat down and the Corner House girl related all that had befallen her since she had left home that morning—save that she said nothing about the mystery of the big album she had found in the Corner House garret, and the Scruggs' interest in its contents.

Her explanation, therefore, as to why the circus clown and his daughter desired to detain her at their camp in the woods was rather hazy; but the fact of the clown being hurt and the helplessness of the two trampers were sufficient to excite the pity and alarm of the farmer and his wife.

"Tut! tut!" clucked Mr. Buckham. "They can't stay out there in the snow. It's going to be mighty cold to-night."

"It is awful to think of," agreed Mrs. Buckham. "But Posey's got her hands full. If I was up and about myself—"

"Oh, dear, Mrs. Buckham! I wasn't thinking of such a thing as bringing them here," Agnes cried. "The man can't walk to the Milton car. He can scarcely walk at all, with that sprained ankle. But if Mr. Buckham will hitch up and drive over there, and take 'em to the car, I can get 'em from the car to the Corner House."

"Oh, dear me, child! To your house?" cried Mrs. Buckham.

"Dunno 'bout that," said Mr. Buckham.

"Of course," said Agnes. "We've plenty of room—and beds enough for a hotel."

"But what will Ruth say?" asked the farmer's wife.

"And what will your Mrs. MacCall say, eh?" chuckled the farmer.

"Why, don't you suppose they will be kind to 'em, too?" cried Agnes. "Ruth would do the same herself. I know these poor folk have very little money and nowhere to go—"

"Enough said, Robert. We have no right to thwart such unselfish impulses," Mrs. Buckham said. "Go and harness up the carriage—"

"No," said the farmer, "I'll take the pung. And I'll fill the body with straw, so 't that poor chap won't get his ankle hurt no more. How's the streets in town, Aggie? How's High Street?"

"Why, it's good sledding," declared the girl. "We see nothing now but automobiles and sleighs."

"Strawberry Farm ain't got quite as fur as an auto yet," chuckled Mr. Buckham. "But maybe we will in time," and he went out to hitch up.

Without having been told further, Posey now brought in a cup of hot cocoa and a nice little luncheon. In the midst of eating this welcome feast, Agnes remembered the forlorn party camping amid the railroad ties.

"Oh, dear me! I don't suppose Mr. Scruggs and Barnabetta have anything at all to eat—poor things!" she cried.

So a big basket was filled with food and a can of coffee, and that Agnes carried out to the sleigh when it appeared at the side porch, and climbed into the great heap of straw with it, and burrowed down. The colts started off briskly, and they left Posey on the porch watching them while Mrs. Buckham waved her hand at the window.

The farmer knew how to drive right to the spot where the Scruggs were encamped, although it was not on his land. When the colts came through the woods, their bells jingling and the snow and ice flying from their sharpened hoofs, Barnabetta appeared suddenly on the pile of ties to see who came.

"Is that the gal?" asked Farmer Buckham of Agnes.

"Yes."

"She's a wild lookin' critter, ain't she?" was Mr. Buckham's comment. "And looks for all the world like a boy!"

Barnabetta disappeared in a moment and when he drew the colts in beside the fire, there she stood with her staff, as though to defend the old clown from the newcomers.

"So you're back again, are you?" was her greeting for Agnes.

"Didn't I tell you I'd bring help?" shouted the Corner House girl, gaily.

"Humph! I don't see what help you can be for the like of us," said the trapeze performer ungraciously.

But Agnes Kenway was not to be balked in her good intentions. "Of course we can help you. I've come to take you home," she declared. "And here's some lunch."

"What d'you mean—home? We haven't got a home, Pop and me."

"But I have," Agnes said.

"That's nothin' to do with us," grumbled Barnabetta.

She looked very sullen and unhappy. The clown was crouching close to the fire, but had drawn his shoe and stocking on again. He looked very miserable, and warm-hearted Agnes determined not to allow herself to become angry with Barnabetta.

"Now, Barnabetta," she said coaxingly, "don't be cross. I want to be friends with you."

"What for?" demanded the other girl, sharply.

"I want to take you to my house," pursued Agnes, without answering the last question. "The Corner House, you know. We've plenty of room and I know my sister, Ruth, will be kind to you."

Barnabetta and her father looked at each other now in stunned surprise. Why Agnes should really want to help them they could not understand.

"Mr. Buckham is kind enough to take us all in his sleigh," pursued Agnes, after calling to Tom Jonah to stay on the other side of the sleigh, for Barnabetta was a little afraid of the big dog. "We'll be in Milton in two hours and there your father can be made comfortable."

"Say! this isn't a trick?" ejaculated the trapeze performer at last.

"What kind of trick?" asked Agnes, in wonder.

"Well," said Barnabetta, doubtfully, "you might make us trouble. We're sort of vagrants. Once, when we were travelin', Pop and me, we got pulled by a fresh constable, and I was afraid they'd find out I wasn't a boy."

"Oh, my!" gasped Agnes, for the romance of Barnabetta's situation appealed strongly to the Corner House girl.

"You're not thinkin' of handin' us over to the police, are you?" added Barnabetta, shrewdly.

"Great goodness, girl!" gasped Mr. Buckham, "it must ha' been your fortune to meet mighty mean folks in your short life."

"Yep, it has," said the circus girl, drily. "We've got plenty good friends in the business. Circus folks are nice folks. Only we got on the outs with the Sorbers.

But outside—well, there's plenty folks down on them that have to tramp it. And we've had our experiences," concluded Barnabetta, nodding her head and pursing her lips.

"Well, these Corner House girls ain't no bad kind," said the farmer, earnestly. "If you need help, you've come to the right shop for it."

"I never asked her for help!" flared up the circus girl.

"You need help just the same," answered Mr. Buckham. "And you'd better take it when it's kindly offered. You know your father ain't in no shape to camp out this weather. And it's getting colder."

"Well," said Barnabetta, ungraciously enough. "What do you say, Pop?"

Poor Scruggs was evidently used to "playing second fiddle," as Mr. Buckham would have himself expressed it. He just nodded, and said:

"I leave it to you, Barney. We'll do just like you say."

The circus girl poised herself on one foot and looked doubtful. Her father did not stir.

"You know," said Agnes, "Neale maybe will be home soon. He'll know how to help you," she added, with confidence in her boy chum's wisdom.

Barnabetta's black eyes suddenly flashed. "All right," she said, grumpily enough, and turned away to help her father rise.

Agnes' heart was suddenly all of a flutter. She could not help wondering if Barnabetta was thinking of the money in the old album that Neale O'Neil was carrying about the country with him. Yet that seemed an ungenerous thought and Agnes put it behind her. Later it was to return in spite of her—and with force.

CHAPTER XVI—SEVERAL ARRIVALS

Perhaps no girl but a Corner House girl would have planned to take two perfect strangers home with her, especially strangers who seemed of a somewhat doubtful character.

It must be confessed that the Corner House girls, with no mother or father to confide in or advise with, sometimes did things on the spur of impulse that ordinary girls would not think of doing.

Agnes Kenway really had serious doubts about the honesty of Barnabetta Scruggs and her father. Just the same she was deeply interested in the circus girl, and she pitied the meek little clown. Barnabetta was quite the most interesting girl Agnes had ever met.

To think of a girl traveling about the country—"tramping it"—dressed as a boy, and so successfully hiding her identity! Why! if she did not speak, nobody would guess her sex, Agnes was sure.

What lots of adventures she must have had! How free and untrammeled her life on the road must be! Agnes herself had often longed for the freedom of trousers. She was jealous of Neale O'Neil because he could do things, and enjoy fun that she could not partake of because of the skirts she wore.

And it was nothing new for the next to the oldest Corner House girl to fall desperately in love with a strange girl at first sight. Neale said, scornfully, that she was forever getting "new spoons." He added that she "had a crush" on some girl almost always; but she seldom kept one of these loves longer than one term of school—sometimes not so long.

Her "very dearest friend" was not always chosen wisely; but while that one was in vogue, Agnes was as loyal to her as ever Damon was to Pythias. And it must be admitted that it was usually by no fault of Agnes' that these friendships were broken off.

For more than one reason did Agnes Kenway contract this sudden and violent fancy for Barnabetta Scruggs.

Neither Mr. nor Mrs. Buckham had raised any objection to Agnes' taking the two strolling people home to the old Corner House, because of two very good reasons. First, they were very simple minded people themselves and it was their rule to do any kindness in their power; and secondly, Agnes had told them nothing at all about the conversation she had overheard between Barnabetta and her father regarding the book filled with money that Neale O'Neil had carried to Tiverton with him.

Agnes helped get the poor circus clown into the straw in the body of the pung. But she sat on the seat with Mr. Buckham when the colts started off along the wood road.

Barnabetta sat down in the straw with her father. Tom Jonah careered about the sleigh and barked. Having seen the two strolling people kindly treated by his little mistress and Mr. Buckham, he gave over being suspicious of them.

The short winter day was drawing to a close. On the rough road Mr. Buckham drove carefully so as not to shake up his passengers, but once they arrived at the more beaten track of the public highway, he let the colts out and they sped swiftly townward.

Agnes was afraid Tom Jonah would be left too far behind and she begged Mr. Buckham to stop so that the old dog might leap into the pung and crouch at their feet in front. He was, indeed, well spent.

"Not that you deserve to be helped at all, Tom Jonah," Agnes said sternly. "You disobeyed—and ran away—and followed me. And I declare you scared me pretty nearly into a fit, so you did!"

But she did not say how glad she was that the big dog had followed her into the wood. His presence had saved her from a very awkward situation. Though what Barnabetta and her father could have done with her had they detained Agnes at their camp, the Corner House girl was unable to imagine. To be a prisoner of the pair of strollers would have been romantic, in Agnes' opinion. But—

"I believe I'd have been a white elephant on their hands, if they'd kept me," she thought, giggling.

The colts swept the party swiftly over the frozen road to the old Corner House. The bells jingled blithely, the runners creaked, the frost and the falling darkness came together; and Agnes, at least, felt highly exhilarated.

How the Scruggses felt she could only suspect. They said nothing. If they were really astonished by this Samaritan act, perhaps they still held doubts regarding the end of the ride.

Mr. Scruggs, however, could not move his foot without pain. It would have been impossible for them to continue their journey to the South with the member in its present condition.

The two circus people had left a local freight at the water-tank that morning, intending to wait for a through freight, running south, that was due late in the evening. They hoped to steal aboard this train—perhaps to pay some small sum to a dishonest brakeman for a ride, and so travel a long way toward their destination before being driven from the train.

With the clown's ankle in its present condition, however, they never could have boarded the train. He and Barnabetta had discussed their circumstances, and were really at their wits' end, when Agnes had returned to them with the farmer and his team.

Whatever may have been their doubts, they could not afford to refuse the help thus proffered them. Even a night in the police station would have been preferable to that which faced them on the snowy hillside overlooking the railroad tracks.

Wonderingly the two strollers arrived at the old Corner House. Willow Street was almost bare of snow; and there was straw laid down there, too. So the farmer brought his team to a stop at the front gate of the Corner House premises.

"Don't try to get out, mister," said Bob Buckham, cordially, "till I tie these critters and blanket 'em. Then I'll help you. You run in and tell your sister she's goin' to have comp'ny," he added to Agnes, saying it that Ruth might have time to adjust her mind to the idea of the strangers coming in.

But this really was not needed, for Ruth was the soul of hospitality. Nor could she ever bear to refuse assistance to those who asked. Had Mrs. MacCall not exercised her shrewd Scotch sense in many cases, the eldest Corner House girl would have been imposed upon by those seeking charity who were quite undeserving.

Having experienced the squeeze of poverty herself, Ruth Kenway knew well what it meant. The generous provision of their guardian, Mr. Howbridge, left a wide margin of money and other means for the Corner House girls to use in a charitable way, if not enough for the automobile that Agnes so heartily craved.

When Asa Scruggs hobbled up to the big front door, leaning on Mr. Buckham on one side and on Barnabetta on the other, the door was wide open, the lamp-light shone out in a broad, cheerful beam across the verandah, and Ruth stood in the doorway to welcome the guests.

The eldest Corner House girl, like her sister, treated the poor clown and his daughter as though they were most honored visitors. Their shabby clothing, their staves, and their bundles done up in blue denim bags, were accepted by Ruth as quite a matter of course.

Visions of the police station and cells evaporated from Barnabetta's active and suspicious brain. This was like entering a fairy castle in a dream!

She and her father stared at each other. They could not understand it. They could barely acknowledge Ruth's pleasantly worded welcome.

"Do come right upstairs, folks," said Agnes, fluttering down the stairway herself, with her hat and coat removed. "I'm so glad you came in, Mr. Buckham. You can help Barnabetta's father up to his room."

"Sure," agreed the farmer.

"Yes," said Ruth. "Unc' Rufus is rheumatically inclined to-day." Then she added to Barnabetta: "You and your father shall be in adjoining rooms. Agnes will show you the bath. And I know you can wear a frock of mine, if you will?"

Barnabetta could hardly speak. She had to swallow something that felt like a big lump in her throat. These girls, without any reason whatever, were treating her as though she were one of themselves. She knew she never would have been so kind to a stranger as they were to her father and herself.

Not only a frock did Barnabetta find laid out in her room a little later—after she had helped her father to bed; but there was linen and underclothing, and even shoes and stockings. And a hot bath was drawn for her in the bathroom with soap and towels laid by. Oh! the forlorn circus girl luxuriated in the bath.

Again and again the girl asked herself why she and the clown were being treated so kindly.

Had Barnabetta known what Agnes had said to Ruth when she ran in ahead of the rest of the party, she might not have been so surprised by Ruth's kindness.

Not a word did the younger girl say about Barnabetta and her father having tried to detain her in the woods.

"Oh, Ruth! these poor folk are circus people. They know Neale O'Neil. And Neale is with his uncle in Tiverton, where he's lying hurt. The circus is in winter quarters there. And the old album is safe!"

She did not say how she knew this last to be the case; and Ruth was so busy making the visitors comfortable that she did not ask, but accepted the good news unquestioningly.

Besides, Ruth had to give some attention to Mr. Bob Buckham. She could allow no guest to be neglected. The old farmer, however, would not stay to dinner.

"That would never do—that would never do!" he declared, when Ruth proposed it. "What would Marm do without me at table? No, sir. I just wanted to see these folks Aggie has taken such a shine to, right to this old Corner House. And say, Ruthie!"

"Yes, sir?" was the girl's response.

"I don't know nothin' about who they be. Nor do you, nor Aggie. So have a care."

"Why, they must be all right, Mr. Buckham," cried Ruth. "Neale knows them. They are from his uncle's circus."

"Eh? Neale knows 'em? Wal—mebbe so, mebbe so," grunted Mr. Buckham. "Just the same, I know lots of folks I wouldn't make too free with. Wait and try 'em out," advised the old farmer.

If Ruth had had any doubts about the trapeze artist and her father, she was at once disarmed when Barnabetta came down to dinner. And Agnes, forgetting her first unpleasant introduction to the strollers in the woods, was delighted with her protégé.

Barnabetta was a dark, glowing beauty. Her curly hair, which made her look so boyish before, framed her thin, striking features most becomingly. Her figure was lithe without being lean.

The little girls, who had not seen Barnabetta arrive in her boy's apparel, were taken with the trapeze artist at once. Agnes had told them what Barnabetta did in the circus, and of course Dot was extremely interested.

"Oh, my!" she said, her eyes shining and her cheeks flushed. "Do—do you climb 'way up on those trapezers at the circus and turn inside outside, just as we saw once? Oh! that must be just heaveningly—mustn't it, Tess?"

Tess was quite as excited over the guest herself, and overlooked Dot's new rendering of certain words for the sake of asking:

"Doesn't it make your head go round and round like a whirligig, to turn over on the trapeze? It does mine, though Neale showed me how to do it on the bar he set up in our garret."

The simple kindness and cordiality of the Corner House girls was a distinct surprise to Barnabetta. At first she showed something of her doubt of this reception she was accorded by such complete strangers. They were all so completely different from her, and their manner of life so entirely strange to her.

The dining room service, the soft lights, the pleasant officiousness of Unc' Rufus, and the girls' own gay conversation, was all a revelation to the circus performer. Even Aunt Sarah Maltby's grim magnificence at her end of the table helped to tame the wildness of Barnabetta Scruggs.

If Mrs. MacCall did not altogether approve of these circus people, she said nothing and did nothing to show such disapproval. Barnabetta began to see that these good folk were very simple and kindly, and wished only to see her at her ease and desired to make her feel at home.

She went back to the clown after dinner, to find that he had been served with a great tray of food by Linda, and lay back among his pillows, happy and content.

Mrs. MacCall had insisted upon looking at his ankle. She bandaged it and anointed it with balsam.

"These folks are mighty good people, Barnabetta," said Asa Scruggs. "I never knowed there were such good folks outside the circus business."

"I don't know what to make of 'em," confessed the girl.

"Don't have to make nothin' of 'em," said her father, with a sigh of content. "This is somethin' to be mighty thankful for. Feel the warm air comin' from that open register, Barnabetta? And I thought we'd haf to scrouge down over a whisp of fire to-night in the open. Oh, my!" and he gave an ecstatic wriggle under the bed clothes.

He seemed ready for sleep, and the girl tiptoed out of the room after turning the gas low. It was while she was in the hall, and before opening the door of her own room, that she heard a sudden subdued hullabaloo below stairs. Listen! what had happened?

Startled, Barnabetta crept along the hall to the front stairway. Somebody had entered by the door from the side porch, bringing in a great breath of keen air that drifted up the stairway to her. The Corner House girls were conducting this new arrival into the sitting room.

"Oh, Neale! you mean thing!" cried Agnes' voice. "Where have you been? Come in and tell us all about it!"

"And what have you done with that old album Agnes let you take?" was Ruth's anxious question.

Barnabetta strained her ears to distinguish the boy's reply.

CHAPTER XVII—AT CROSS PURPOSES

Tess had been over to see how Sammy Pinkney was after dinner. That was her usual evening task now. She would go into the Pinkney yard and yodle.

"Ee-yow! ee-yow! ee-yow!" That was the way in which Sammy himself usually announced his coming to the old Corner House, and Tess had learned it from him.

Then Mrs. Pinkney would come to the side door to speak to the little girl.

"How is Sammy to-night, Mrs. Pinkney?" Tess would query. "We hope he's better."

And Mrs. Pinkney would tell her. In the morning on her way to school, Tess would repeat the inquiry. For a week the reports were very grave indeed. Sammy knew nobody—not even his father and mother. The poor little "pirate" was quite delirious; his temperature was very high; and Dr. Forsyth could give the parents little encouragement.

But this evening, for the first time, Tess' shrill little "Ee-yow! ee-yow! ee-yow!" was heard by the boy inside, and recognized. Mrs. Pinkney came running to the door.

"I do wish I dared run out and kiss you, Tessie Kenway!" she cried, and there were tears of thankfulness in her eyes. "Sammy heard you. He's better. Bless you, dear! He is better. Yodle for him again."

So Tess did, and right away there was an unexpected answer. Somebody repeated "Ee-yow! ee-yow! ee-yow!" behind her in Willow Street.

"Goodness gracious!" squealed Tess, running wildly out of the gate, "is that you, Neale O'Neil?"

"That's who it is, honey," said the white-haired boy, cheerfully.

"Oh, Neale! so much has happened since you've been gone. Sammy's got scarlet fever; but he's better. And Almira's got four kittens. And we've got visitors, and one of 'em's a girl and she can turn on the trapeze—so easy! And you've got a whole heap of Christmas presents in the sitting room that you've never seen yet."

"All right. I'll go in and see 'em right now," Neale said, and took her hand in his free one. When they mounted the porch steps and Agnes and Ruth and Dot came running to the door to meet him, he dropped his heavy bag in a corner and did not take it into the house. He had just come from the railroad station.

"You see," Neale said, when he was hustled into the warm sitting room by the four Corner House girls, and even before he took off his coat and cap and gloves, "I got a letter about Uncle Bill Sorber from one of the other Sorbers. He was hurt two months ago—badly burned, poor old fellow!—when the circus arrived at winter quarters.

"They always give a last performance there at Tiverton, and another when they start out in the spring. There was an accident this time. A tank of gasoline fell from aloft, and got afire, and Uncle Bill was hurt badly. The doctors gave him up at last, and so they sent for me."

"I know about it," said Agnes, nodding.

"How'd you know? Must have seen it in the paper, I s'pose," said Neale. "Well, I missed it. I didn't know a thing about his being hurt till I found that letter at home Christmas Eve."

"But why did you go away without telling us?" Ruth asked earnestly.

"I didn't want to bother you girls, then. And you expected me to help you at that Christmas tree business, too. So I only left the note with Unc' Rufus and told him not to give it to you till just before dinner. I fixed it with Con Murphy to take my place. He did, didn't he?"

"Yes," the eager Agnes said.

The little girls had danced off to the kitchen on some errand. The boy continued:

"Well! I got up there to the winter quarters and found Uncle Bill better. But the poor old fellow had been asking for me. I don't suppose we ever will understand each other," sighed Neale. "He can't see why I want to be something different from a circus performer; and an education doesn't mean a thing to him but foolishness.

"But I guess he really does have some interest in me—"

"Of course he does, Neale," interposed Ruth, admonishingly. "I could tell that the time he was here and I talked with him."

"Just the same, I wish I had money myself, so's not to have to take any from him," the boy said stubbornly.

"Well," burst out Ruth, "you have had plenty of money with you lately, Neale O'Neil, whether you know it or not! What under the sun have you done with that great old book Aggie found in the garret?"

"Oh, mercy, yes, Neale!" put in Agnes. "What did you do with it? Ruth's just about worried her heart and soul out about it."

"What for?" asked Neale, flushing deeply.

"Well, goodness!" cried Agnes. "I believe that Ruth believes that old book is full of money."

"What of it?" asked Neale, still looking red and angry.

"Why, Neale, we'd like to know what you've done with it," Ruth said, seriously. "Aggie had no right to let you take the book."

"Why not?" snapped the boy again.

"Because it was not hers. It does not belong to us. It should not have gone out of my care. It—"

"Well! why didn't you take care of it, then?" demanded the boy, sharply.

"I—I didn't know what was in it. I couldn't believe it!" declared Ruth, with clasped hands.

"For pity's sake! what is the matter with you, Ruth Kenway?" cried Agnes, feeling that they were all at cross purposes. "If it was real money or counterfeit, either one, of course Neale was to be trusted with it, I should hope."

"If!" ejaculated Ruth, desperately. "You don't know what you say, Agnes. There's no 'if' about it. It is real money."

"No?" gasped the astounded Agnes, who had never really believed this was so. "How do you know that, Ruth Kenway? It is preposterous."

"It is so," repeated Ruth, more calmly. "I took one of the ten dollar bills and had it examined at the bank. Mr. Crouch says it is good money. I didn't believe it myself till he said so. Then I came back to find the book and lock it away somewhere. And you had given it to Neale."

"Oh, Neale!" gasped Agnes, sitting down suddenly.

"Well! what if I did have it? And what if it is good money?" repeated the white-haired boy, still standing as though on the defensive. "Do you think I'd run away with it, Ruth Kenway?"

"You did go away with it, didn't you?" returned Ruth, a little sharp herself, now. "I have been worried to death."

"But of course it's all right," Agnes hastened to put in, trying to throw oil on the troubled waters. "You brought the old album back with you, didn't you, Neale?"

"Yes, I did," Neale admitted. "But I'd like to know what Ruth means by what she says. If there had been a hundred thousand dollars in that book do you s'pose I'd steal it?"

"A hundred thousand dollars!" murmured Agnes. "Oh—dear—me!"

"I didn't know what to think," Ruth said slowly. "I have worried—oh! so much!" and she sobbed.

"Because I carried away that old book?" repeated Neale.

"Yes. Oh! it would have been just the same if anybody had carried it off. I don't know who all that fortune belongs to; but we must take care of it till Mr. Howbridge comes."

"Oh, my goodness me!" squealed Agnes. "Is it true? Can it be so? All—that—money?"

"I'm sure it isn't ours," Ruth said quietly. "Uncle Peter never hid away any such sum. He wasn't as rich as all that. But we've got to give an account of it to somebody."

"What for?" demanded her sister. "I found it."

"But findings isn't always keepings, Aggie—especially where so much money is concerned. A hundred thousand dollars!"

"A hundred thousand dollars!" repeated Agnes, in the same awed tone.

Neale pulled his cap tighter down over his ears. It was an angry gesture.

"Where are you going, Neale?" demanded Ruth, exasperated. "Do sit down and tell us what you have done. Don't you see we are anxious? I never saw such a boy! Do tell us!"

"I don't know why I should tell you anything," returned the boy, grumpily enough. "You think I'm a thief. I won't stay here."

"Oh, Neale!" shrieked Agnes, seeing how serious this difference was. "Don't get mad."

"Let him return the book," said Ruth, insistently. "This isn't any foolish matter, I assure you. He has no right to keep it."

"Did I say I was going to keep it?" flared out Neale O'Neil.

"Well, you have kept it. You carried it away to Tiverton, you say," went on Ruth, accusingly.

"Well, so I did," admitted Neale.

"What for, I'd like to know?" demanded the oldest Corner House girl in exasperation.

"I lugged it along to show to somebody."

"What for—if you didn't think it was good money?"

"Oh, Ruth!" begged Agnes again. "Don't!"

"I want him to answer," cried her elder sister, severely. "Why did he carry the album away? And where is it now?"

It must be confessed that Ruth Kenway had worked herself into a fever of excitement. It was the result of the repressed anxiety she had so long endured regarding this strange and wonderful find of Agnes' in the old Corner House garret.

Neale was very pale now. He was usually slow to anger, and his friends, the Corner House girls, had never seen him moved so deeply before.

"I did think the bonds might be worth something," Neale said, at last, and hoarsely. "I told Aggie so."

"But the money?" cried Ruth.

"You say it's good," the boy returned. "You can believe that's so if you want to. I didn't think it was when I took the book."

"I tell you Mr. Crouch, at the bank, said it was perfectly good. See here!" cried Ruth, desperately.

She ran for her purse that lay on the sewing-machine table. She opened it and drew forth the folded ten dollar bill. With it came the other bill she had put away.

"I showed him this!" Ruth began, when Agnes stooped to pick up the other.

"What's this?" the second sister asked.

"Why—why that's the one Mr. Howbridge gave me. I haven't needed to break it."

"And you had 'em both together?" demanded Agnes, shrewdly.

"Yes."

"Which one did you show Mr. Crouch then?"

The question stunned Ruth for the moment. She unfolded the bill she had taken out of the purse. It was quite a new silver certificate. Agnes unfolded the other. It was an old-style United States banknote, dated long before the girls' parents were born.

Neale, as well as the Kenway sisters, saw the significance of the discovery. The boy turned his face aside quickly and so hid the smile that automatically wreathed his lips.

"Why—why!" gasped Agnes, "if you showed Mr. Crouch that bill, of course he said it was a good one. But how about this?"

Ruth turned like a flash on Neale again. "What do you know about the money in the book? Isn't it good?" she demanded. "I believe you've found out."

"Well! what if I have?" and one would hardly recognize Neale O'Neil's pleasant voice in the snarling tone that now answered the oldest Corner House girl.

"Oh, Neale! is it?" cried Agnes.

But Neale gave her no reply. He was still glaring at Ruth whose expression of her doubt of his honesty had rasped the boy's temper till he fairly raged.

"If you want to find out anything about that stuff in the old book, you can do it yourself. I won't tell you. I'm through with the whole business," declared Neale.

"But—but where's the book?" asked Ruth, in rather a weak voice now.

"Oh, I brought it back," snapped Neale. "You'll find it outside on the porch—in my bag. That's all I carried in the old thing, anyway. You can have it."

He marched to the door and jerked it open. Agnes tried to call after him, but could not.

Neale banged to the door behind him and tramped down the hall. They heard him open the outer door and slam that. Then he thumped down the steps and made for the Willow Street gate.

"Oh, Ruth! what have you done?" gasped Agnes, wringing her hands. "Poor Neale!"

"I want that album!" exclaimed Ruth, jumping up.

"It—it can't be worth anything—that money," murmured Agnes, but followed her sister.

"It is good money. I'm sure of it!" snapped Ruth.

She hurried to the porch. There was Neale's old bag in the dark corner. Ruth pounced upon it.

"Oh, Ruth!" cried Agnes. "It's never there."

"Yes, it is. He didn't stop when he went out. Of course it's here!"

Ruth had brought the satchel into the lighted hall and opened it. She turned it upside down and shook it.

But nothing shook out—not a thing. The bag was empty. The old album Agnes had found in the garret, and which had caused all their worry and trouble, had disappeared from Neale's satchel.

CHAPTER XVIII—WHAT HAPPENED IN THE NIGHT

The two youngest Corner House girls had heard nothing of this exciting discussion in the sitting room between Neale O'Neil and their two older sisters.

Tess and Dot had run to tell the rest of the family that Neale had arrived and that Sammy Pinkney was better. Mrs. MacCall, who had a soft spot in her heart for the white-haired boy, put down some supper to warm for him, sure that Neale would come into the kitchen before he went home.

Dot ran upstairs to Aunt Sarah Maltby's room to tell her of the boy's arrival, and Aunt Sarah actually expressed her satisfaction that he had reached home in safety. Neale was growing slowly in the brusk old lady's good graces.

Coming downstairs and through the dining room, where the gas-logs blazed cheerfully on the hearth, Dot found Sandyface, the "grandmother" cat, crouching close before the blaze, her forepaws tucked in, and expressing her satisfaction at the warmth and comfort in a manner very plain to be heard.

"Mercy me!" ejaculated the smallest Corner House girl. "Sandyface! you sound just as though you were beginning to boil! Oh!"

For just then the door from the rear hall opened quickly and startled her. The strange girl—the circus girl—who had so interested Dot and Tess, to say nothing of the rest of the family, popped in.

"Oh!" repeated Dot. "How you frightened me."

Barnabetta stood with her back against the door. One might have thought that the appearance of Dot, had been quite as unexpected and had frightened her.

She seemed breathless, too, as though she had been running. But of course she had not been running. Where should she have run to on such a cold night? And there was no snow on her shoes. Besides, she wore no wrap.

"Did—did I frighten you, little girl?" Barnabetta said. "I am sorry, I did not mean to."

She had both hands behind her and stood against the door in a most awkward position.

"I was afraid you had gone to bed," prattled on Dot, stroking Sandyface. "Ruthie said she s'posed you had. But I'm glad you hadn't. I wanted to ask you something."

"Did—did you?" returned Barnabetta. She seemed to be listening all the time—as though something was going on in the hall that frightened her.

"Yes," Dot went on placidly. "You know, we've been to a circus once."

"Is that so?"

"Yes. And Tess and I was awful int'rested in it. We—we liked the ladies and gentlemans that rode on the horses around the ring, and was on the trapezers, too. And they looked beau-tiful in those spangles, and velvets, and all."

"I s'pose those were their best clo'es, weren't they—their real, Sunday-go-to-meeting frocks?"

"I—I guess they were," admitted Barnabetta.

"You wear your best clo'es when you go up on the trapezers, don't you?"

"The fanciest I've got," admitted the circus girl.

"Well! Mustn't they look funny all going to church that way—the ladies in those short, fluffy skirts, and the gentlemans in such tight pants! My!" gasped Dot. "Couldn't you tell us, please, what they do in circuses when they travel?"

"Why—yes," said Barnabetta. "I'll tell you."

"Will you sit right down here and tell us?"

"Why—yes."

"Oh, wait! I'll run and fetch Tess!" exclaimed the generous Dot. "I know she will want to hear, too," and she scampered out of the room so swiftly that she startled Sandyface, who flew through the door before her.

Barnabetta was left alone in the dining room. There was a closet with a small door right beside the fireplace. When Dot returned with Tess the circus girl was leaning her back against that closet door, instead of against the hall door.

"Oh, do come and sit down," urged Dot, eagerly, drawing an armchair to the hearth.

Barnabetta did so. Tess and Dot each brought a hassock, one on either side of the older girl. Barnabetta had a softer side to her nature than the side she had displayed to Agnes Kenway. There were little folk at the circus, who traveled with their parents with the show, who loved Barnabetta Scruggs.

A little later Agnes, pale of face and with traces of tears, came into the room. She and Ruth had hunted high and low for the lost album Neale O'Neil had left in his satchel on the side porch.

Even Ruth admitted Neale had not halted there, when he went out so angrily, long enough to take the album away. And both girls had seen him drop the heavy bag in that dark corner when he came in with Tess.

Somebody had removed the album. Nor was it ridiculous to suppose that the "somebody" who had done this knew very well what the book contained.

"Oh, we've been robbed! robbed!" Ruth had cried, rocking herself back and forth in her chair in the sitting room. "What ever shall we do? What shall I say to Mr. Howbridge?"

"I don't care a thing about him," declared Agnes, recklessly. "But think of all that money—if it is money—"

"I tell you it is."

"But you don't know for sure," Agnes retorted. "Maybe you showed Mr. Crouch the wrong bill."

"No. I've felt all the time," Ruth said despairingly, "that we really had a great fortune in our hands. How it came to be hidden in our garret, I don't know. Whom it really belongs to I don't know."

"Us! We found it!" sobbed Agnes.

"No. We cannot claim it. At least, not until we have searched for the rightful owners. But Mr. Howbridge will tell us."

"Oh! mercy me, Ruthie Kenway!" cried Agnes. "What's the use of talking? It's go-o-one!"

"I don't know who—"

"You can't blame Neale now!" flared up Agnes. "You've made him mad, too. He'll never forgive us."

"Well! What business had he to carry off that book?" demanded Ruth. "He can be mad if he wants to be. If he hadn't carried it away there would have been no trouble at all."

"Oh, Ruthie! It isn't his fault that somebody has stolen it now," repeated Agnes.

"Why isn't it?"

"How could it be?"

"Like enough the foolish boy showed all that money to somebody, and he has been followed right here to the house by the robber."

Agnes gasped. Then she sat back in her chair and stared at her sister. Suddenly, with an inarticulate cry, she arose and dashed upstairs.

Although she had not asked, Agnes supposed the circus girl had retired immediately after dinner. It was still early in the evening, and Agnes and Ruth had had no private conversation regarding Barnabetta and her father. Neale's arrival had driven that out of both their minds.

But into Agnes' brain now came the thought that Barnabetta had seen the old album full of money and bonds while Neale was at the winter quarters of the circus.

"Oh, dear me! Can she be so very, very wicked?" thought Agnes. "They are so desperately in need. And such an amount of money is an awful temptation— that is, it would be a temptation if it were money!"

For despite all that Ruth said, Agnes could not believe that the wonderful contents of the old album was bona fide money and bonds.

The thought, however, that Barnabetta might be tempted to steal from those who had been kind to her, troubled Agnes exceedingly. She did not want to say anything to Ruth about her suspicions of the circus girl yet. Why make her sister suspicious, too, unless she was sure of her evidence?

Agnes listened at the door of Barnabetta's room. There was no sound in there and she finally turned the knob softly and pushed open the door a crack. The lighted room was revealed; but there was no sign of occupancy save the shabby boy's clothing folded on a chair. The bed had not been touched.

Was the circus girl with her father? Or had she left the house on some errand?

Agnes crept to the other door and put her ear to the panel. At first she heard nothing. Then came a murmur, as of voices in low conversation. Were the circus people talking? Had Barnabetta really gained possession of the book, and were she and her father examining it?

Then Agnes suddenly fell to giggling; for what she actually heard was Mr. Asa Scruggs' rhythmic snoring.

"She surely isn't there," decided Agnes, creeping away down the hall again. "He's sound asleep. If Barnabetta's up to any mischief—if she's taken that album—she can't be in there with it."

It was immediately following this decision that Agnes, returning downstairs by the front way, heard voices in the dining room. She looked in to see Barnabetta sitting with Tess and Dot before the fire, telling the little girls stories of circus life.

Agnes dodged out of there. She had seen enough, she thought, to convince any one that the circus girl was not guilty.

"Where'd you go to?" demanded Ruth, when her sister returned to the sitting room.

"I went to see where that Barnabetta Scruggs was," confessed Agnes.

"Oh, my! I did not think of them." Ruth said.

"Well, she's all right. She's in the dining room telling Tess and Dot stories. It certainly could not be Barnabetta. Why! we'd have heard her go through the hall and out upon the porch."

"Why! She doesn't know anything about the album," retorted Ruth. "I tell you it's been stolen by somebody who followed Neale here to the house."

"Well, surely that couldn't be Barnabetta," admitted Agnes; "for she got here first."

"That is true," Ruth agreed. "No. Somebody followed that foolish boy—perhaps away from Tiverton. And to think of his throwing down a satchel of money on the porch in that careless way!"

"Oh, but Ruthie! that proves Neale doesn't believe it is good money," Agnes said eagerly. "Else he wouldn't have left it out there. Of course he has found out that it is all counterfeit."

"You never can tell what a foolish boy will do," retorted Ruth, tossing her head.

"Shall—shall we tell the police we've been robbed?" hesitated Agnes.

"Why should we tell them, I'd like to know?" demanded Ruth, shortly. "What should we tell them? That we've lost a hundred thousand dollars that doesn't belong to us?"

"Oh, mercy!"

"I'd be afraid to," confessed the troubled Ruth. "You don't know what they might do to us for losing it."

"Oh, dear, Ruthie! that sounds awful," murmured Agnes.

The two girls were in much vexation of spirit, and quite uncertain what to do. The emergency called for wisdom beyond that which they possessed. Nor did they know anybody at hand with whom they might confer regarding the catastrophe.

Agnes wanted to run after Neale and ask his opinion. He might know, or at least suspect, who it was that had taken the album out of the satchel.

But Ruth would not hear of taking Neale into their affairs further. She was quite put out with their boy friend. And Agnes, from past experience, knew that when Ruth was in this present mood it was no use to argue with her.

They spent a very unhappy evening indeed. The two oldest Corner House girls, that is. As for Tess and Dot, they reveled till bedtime in a new and wonderful world—the circus world.

They listened to Barnabetta tell of long journeys through the country, when the big animals, like the camels and the elephants, marched by night, and the great cages and pole-wagons and tent-wagons, rumbled over the roads from one "stand" to another. Of adventures on the way. Of accidents when wagons broke down, or got into sloughs. Sometimes cages burst open when the accidents occurred, and some of the animals got out.

"Oh, dear, me!" cried Tess, so excited that she could scarcely sit still. "To think of lions, and tigers, and panthers running loose!"

"What's a 'panther,' sister?" queried Dot, puzzled. "Are panthers dangerous?"

"Very," responded Tess, wisely. "Of course."

"Why—why, I didn't s'pose that was so," murmured Dot.

"For pity's sake!" Tess exclaimed, exasperated. "What do you s'pose a panther is, anyway, Dot Kenway?"

"Why—why," stammered the smallest Corner House girl, "I—I thought a panther was a man who made pants."

"Oh, goodness to gracious, Miss Barnabetta! Did you ever hear of such a child?" demanded Tess, hopelessly. "She never will learn the English language!"

Ruth came all too quickly to remind the little girls that it was bedtime. Although much troubled, the oldest Corner House girl did not forget their guests' comfort.

Mr. Scruggs was settled for the night and Barnabetta was sure he would not need anything before morning. She accepted a cup of hot cocoa and a biscuit herself and took them up stairs with her. Agnes did not appear again, and Barnabetta did not know that she was being watched by a pair of troubled blue eyes from the darker end of the hall.

Agnes had Barnabetta very much in her mind. She and Ruth agreed to say nothing in their own room about the mysterious disappearance of the album. The door was open into the children's room and it was notorious that "little pitchers have big ears."

After they were in bed, Agnes still lay and thought about Barnabetta. Was it possible that the circus girl had obtained possession of the mysterious old album?

It seemed ridiculous to believe such a thing. Surely she had not removed it to her room, for Agnes had been there and had looked for it. Barnabetta had been quietly telling stories to Tess and Dot downstairs all the evening.

Yet, the very fact that the circus girl was downstairs troubled Agnes. Suppose she had come down while Neale and Ruth and she, Agnes, were talking so excitedly about the odd find that had been made in the garret? Suppose Barnabetta had heard most of their talk?

"Easy enough for her to have slipped out of the door and grabbed that old book," murmured Agnes. "But then—what did she do with it? Oh, dear me! How awful of me to suspect her of such wickedness."

In the midst of her ruminations she heard a doorlatch click. The house had long since become still. It was very near midnight.

Agnes sat up in bed and strained her ears to catch the next sound. But there seemed to be no further movement. Had somebody left one of the bedrooms, or was it a draught that had shaken the door?

The uncertainty of this got upon the girl's nerves. Somebody might be creeping downstairs. Suppose it were Barnabetta?

"What would she go down again for?" Agnes asked herself.

Yet even as she thought this and how ridiculous it was, she crept out of bed. Ruth was sound asleep. Nobody heard Agnes as she felt around with her bare feet and got them into her fleece-lined bedroom slippers. Then, wrapping her robe about her, she tied the cord and found her bedroom candle.

She lit this and went out into the hall, the door being open. As she came noiselessly to the top of the main stairway she saw the reflection of another candle on the ceiling above the stairwell—a bobbing reflection that showed somebody was moving slowly down the lower flight.

Agnes, not daring to breathe audibly, shielded her own light with her free hand, and hastened to peer over the balustrade.

CHAPTER XIX—THE KEY TO THE CLOSET

Agnes was too late to see who it was at the foot of the front stairs. As she craned her head over the railing guarding the gallery above, the person with the candle went into the dining room.

This mysterious individual must have found the door open. There was no clicking of a latch down there. The figure had glided into the room with the candle, and was immediately out of sight.

"Just as silent as a ghost!" breathed Agnes. "Oh!"

She almost giggled aloud, for she remembered the time when—oh! so very long ago—the Corner House family had been troubled by a ghost in the garret—or, as Dot seemed determined to call it, "a goat."

Ghost or no ghost, Agnes felt that she had to see this thing through. Even a disembodied spirit had no right to go wandering about the old Corner House at night with a lighted bedroom candle in its hand.

She ran lightly downstairs, still sheltering the flame of her own candle with her hand. The dining room door had been pushed quietly to; but it was not latched.

Hiding her candle so that it should not shine through the crack of the door, Agnes pushed the portal open again with her free hand. There was a glimmer of light ahead.

The dining room was a large apartment. The candle in the hand of the unknown made only a blur of light at the far end of the room.

What was the bearer of the candle about? At first Agnes could not discover. The candle was near the door which opened into the hall near the side porch door. Through that hall one could easily reach the dark corner where Neale O'Neil had thrown his satchel when he arrived at the old Corner House that evening.

A number of thoughts were buzzing in Agnes Kenway's brain. In spite of herself she was unable to disconnect thought of Barnabetta Scruggs and the missing book of money and bonds. It might be that the circus girl had descended the stairs and, listening at the sitting room door while Neale was there, had heard what he said about the old book; and so slipped out and stolen the album either just before Neale flung himself out of the house, or just afterward. There would have been time to do so in either case.

If Barnabetta knew nothing about the missing album, why was she creeping about the house at this unearthly hour? The question seemed, to Agnes' mind, to be unanswerable save as the answer fitted the above probabilities.

"But I don't really know that this is Barnabetta," Agnes' excusing self objected.

She did not wish it to be the circus girl. As much as she desired to know what had become of the album, she did not wish to find it in Barnabetta Scruggs' possession.

The candle in the hand of the figure Agnes followed was suddenly raised higher. The Corner House girl jumped and almost uttered a sharp exclamation aloud. Why! Barnabetta was not as tall as that!

This ghostly visitor to the dining room was an adult. She saw its flowing robe now. The candle, held so high, threw the shadow of the head on the wall in sharp relief.

"Her hair's done up in a 'pug' behind," gasped Agnes. "Who can it be? Mrs. MacCall, or—or Aunt Sarah?"

The mysterious person was at the closet built into the brickwork of the chimney-piece, not at the hall door. That closet was a catch-all for all manner of odds and ends. There were shelves up high, as well as a deep bin underneath.

Agnes felt she must know who the person was who was rummaging in the closet, and what she was about. She softly extinguished her own candle, and set it down on the floor in the hall. Then she pushed the door open wider and ventured into the dining room.

"Aunt Sarah!"

Agnes did not utter this ejaculation aloud; but she was completely surprised.

The grim looking old woman was fumbling on the top shelf of the cupboard, and she was muttering to herself in a most exasperated tone.

"Those dratted young ones are into everything!" was Aunt Sarah's complaint. "A body can't find a thing put away as it should be."

She stepped back from the cupboard then. She closed the door with an angry snap, and then stood, meditating.

Agnes had darted around the big table and crouched down. Aunt Sarah half turned from the closet door; then she turned back again.

Was the old lady asleep or awake? Agnes did not know that Aunt Sarah ever walked in her sleep. But she knew that somnambulists did very strange things, and, of course, Aunt Sarah might be a sleep-walker.

Aunt Sarah Maltby proceeded to do a very strange thing now. There was a heavy brass key in the lock of the cupboard door. The old lady suddenly turned the key, locked the door, withdrew the key, and, clutching it tightly in her hand, marched back toward the front hall door.

It was just at this moment that Agnes Kenway was treated to a second surprise. She suddenly realized that there was a third person in the room!

It was because of no movement upon the part of the mysterious third person that Agnes made this exciting discovery. But she heard a quick sigh, or intake of breath, somewhere at the lower end of the room near the pantry door. She thought of Tom Jonah first of all; but then remembered that the old dog had gone out at bedtime and had not come in again.

Most exciting thoughts raced through Agnes Kenway's brain. She had followed Aunt Sarah downstairs and into the dining room. But had Aunt Sarah followed somebody else here, at midnight?

"What under the sun is going on?" was Agnes' muttered comment. "My goodness! I wish Ruth were here. Or Neale!"

The Corner House girl felt very much disturbed indeed. She did not believe in ghosts; but she did believe in burglars!

At that moment all thought of Barnabetta Scruggs went out of Agnes' troubled mind. Aunt Sarah passed out of the dining room door into the front hall and closed the door carefully behind her. This left the great room in perfect darkness.

Agnes was actually trembling with excitement and fear. She had not thought to be afraid at all until she heard that mysterious sigh. The fact that she had no means of identifying the midnight marauder increased her fright.

There it was again—a short intake of breath! Somebody was surely hiding at the lower end of the room. Agnes must have come into the room so quietly that the unknown person did not apprehend her presence.

Fearful as she was, Agnes did not move. If her presence was not already discovered she had no intention whatever of revealing it to the unknown.

There was suddenly a faint sound, as of a clumsily shod foot striking against one of the heavy chairs. Agnes could see nothing at first; but she seemed actually to feel the moving presence at the lower end of the room.

There are degrees of darkness just as there are of light. Something darker—or more solid—than the atmosphere of the dining room, passed across the line of Agnes' vision.

The moving figure approached the cupboard in the chimney-place. Agnes knew that the unknown person stood just where Aunt Sarah had stood shortly before.

A tentative hand shook the closet door gently. It rattled; but the old lock was a strong one. Nothing less than a crowbar or a burglar's jimmy could have forced that door.

Evidently the mysterious marauder was not armed with either of these implements. Agnes heard a sigh that was almost a sob! Then she knew that the disappointed unknown had turned hopelessly from the closet door.

Whatever it was this person wanted, Aunt Sarah had locked it up in the cupboard and carried away the key.

Agnes, crouching beyond the table, realized that the visitor glided to the door leading into the back hall. The door was opened. For a single instant the figure was partially revealed in outline to the girl's straining vision.

It was the figure of a man!

Then the door closed on its exit. Agnes sprang to her feet. Had the unknown one not closed the door, he must have heard her then, for Agnes was too excited by her last discovery to be at all careful.

"A man! A man in the house!" thought the terrified girl. And then, remarking a single peculiarity of the mysterious figure, she whispered: "Not a man, but a boy. Goodness! who can it be?"

Quick as a flash Agnes Kenway ran to the door leading into the front hall, by which she had entered. She opened it and slipped into the hall. Neglecting her candle which she had placed on the floor for safety, she crept back toward the darker end of the hall.

There was an "elbow" in the passage behind the front stairway and she could not see beyond this. But she heard a sound—the unmistakable sound of a bolt being drawn.

Was the mysterious visitor at the porch door? Was he leaving the house? And how had he got in?

Agnes waited breathlessly for some further noise. But there was none.

Five minutes passed. Then ten. The seconds were being ticked off in a ghostly fashion by the tall clock behind her.

Agnes crouched in the corner and trembled. Usually she was brave; but the experiences of the last half hour had gotten upon the girl's nerves.

At last she could remain quiet no longer. She stole to the rear of the dark hall— past the sitting room door and beyond leading into the dining room, and through which the boy had passed.

This end of the passage was comparatively narrow. Agnes could be sure that nobody was hiding here, for some light filtered down the back stairway from the floor above.

Before her was the door of the porch. She fumbled for the knob, and found it. She opened the door easily. This was the bolt she had heard drawn.

Here Agnes suffered the very worst scare of the whole adventure. Something cold and wet was thrust against her hand!

She almost screamed aloud. She would have screamed, only the fright of it made her lose her voice. She swung there, clinging to the doorknob, about to fall fainting to the floor, when a bulky object pushed by her and she heard Tom Jonah's whine.

"Oh! You dear, old, foolish, mean, silly thing!" gasped Agnes. "How you scared me. I'll never forgive you, Tom Jonah! But I'm so glad it's only you."

This she whispered, while she hugged the shaggy dog. Tom Jonah had evidently found it too cold for comfort outside the house, and hearing her at the door had come to beg entrance for the night.

She let him into the kitchen and then, as she went back to the door, she was suddenly smitten with this thought:

"If that boy went out of that door, Tom Jonah must have known him!"

The old dog had known him so well that he made no objection to his being about the old Corner House. There was but one boy in the world whom Tom Jonah would allow to do such a thing. That was Neale O'Neil.

The thought gave Agnes Kenway a feeling of dire dismay. She could not understand it. She could not believe it.

Yet she was sure the boy had gone out by this door. But how he had first got into the house was a mystery beyond her divination.

At once she shot the bolt again. Once out, the youthful marauder, whoever he was, should stay out, as far as this particular means of entrance was concerned.

"It couldn't be a real burglar," murmured Agnes, quiveringly. "Oh, Neale! I wouldn't have thought it of you!

"And Aunt Sarah must have scared him when he was at that closet. But, goodness me! what would Neale O'Neil want in that old closet? Nothing there much but medicines on the top shelf and old books and papers. I—don't see—

"Could it be a really, truly burglar, after all? Not one like Dot's plumber, but a real one? And why didn't Tom Jonah bark? Oh, goodness! suppose he hasn't gone out after all?

"Oh! I want to go to bed and cover my head up with blankets!" gasped Agnes. "I want to tell Ruth—but I daren't! Maybe I ought to call everybody and make a search for the burglar. But suppose it should be Neale?"

So she stole up to bed, shaking with nervous dread, yet feeling as though she ought, somehow, to be congratulated. Yet when she had slipped off her robe and was in bed again, two separate and important thoughts assailed her:

Had Barnabetta Scruggs been out of her room? And what had Aunt Sarah Maltby done with the key to the dining room closet?

CHAPTER XX—LEMUEL ADEN'S DIARY

Agnes slept so late that Sunday morning that she had to "scrabble," as she herself confessed, to get down to breakfast before everybody else was through.

As the members of the Corner House family who had risen earlier made no remarks about burglars in the night, Agnes decided she would better say nothing of her own experience.

It really seemed to Agnes now as though it had been a dream. Only she noticed when she sat down at the table that the big brass key was missing from the lock of the closet door.

Aunt Sarah said nothing at that time about her midnight rambling; nor about what she had locked up in the chimney-place cupboard. Ruth looked much worried and disturbed. Of course, the missing album had not come to light. Ruth truly believed that a great fortune had been within their grasp and it was now utterly gone.

"And gone beyond redemption. We shall never see it again," she said to Agnes.

Agnes did not want to discuss this with her sister. She was quite as puzzled as was Ruth over the disappearance of the old album in which had been pasted the bonds and money; only she could not bring herself to believe, as Ruth did, that the bonds and money were good.

She wondered if Neale O'Neil had found the answer to this problem while he was in Tiverton. Then she winced when she thought of Neale. He did not appear at the old Corner House on this Sunday morning, as he usually did.

They must wait until Monday for Ruth to go to the bank again and have the right ten dollar bill examined. She admitted that she might have shown the new banknote instead of the old one to Mr. Crouch.

"Though lots of good it will do us to know for certain whether the money was good and legal tender or not, now that it has been stolen," Ruth grieved.

Barnabetta appeared at breakfast and Agnes noticed that the circus girl's eyes were red and her manner much subdued.

The Corner House family prepared for church much as usual. Aunt Sarah always made most of her preparations—even to the filling of her dress pocket with a handful of peppermint lozenges—the night before.

Time was when the Kenway sisters had to scrimp and save to find the five pennies weekly to purchase Aunt Sarah's supply of peppermints; now they were bought in quantity and—

"I don't see why you young ones can't leave 'em alone," said the old lady, severely, as she swept down into the hall in her best silk dress and popped the first lozenge of the day into her mouth.

"I forgot 'em last night till I'd got to bed, and when I come down here for 'em, I declare I couldn't scurce find 'em in that cupboard. But I got 'em locked away now an' I guess you won't be so free with 'em."

At this Agnes was attacked by "a fit of the giggles," as Aunt Sarah expressed it. But the girl was not laughing at Aunt Sarah. Her thought was:

"My goodness me! was that what the burglar was after—Aunt Sarah's peppermints?" But she missed seeing Barnabetta's face at this juncture.

Dot cried: "Oh, my, Miss Barnabetta! don't you feel well a-tall this morning?"

"Oh, yes, my dear, I am quite well," said the circus girl, hastily.

Tess said doubtfully: "I—I hope we didn't tire you last night asking for stories?"

"No, indeed."

"But you just did look as though you were going to faint," said Dot.

"There, there," said Mrs. MacCall. "Appearances aren't everything. The looks of a toad don't tell how far he's goin' to hop."

"No-o," agreed Tess. "And, anyway, toads are very useful animals, even if they are so very ugly."

Barnabetta had the two little girls again, one on either side of her, before the fire. She had plainly become their fast friend.

Barnabetta said, more cheerfully: "Toads are not always ugly. Didn't you ever see a toad early in the mornin'—when the grass and everything is all sparklin' with dew? Oh! I must tell you a story about that."

"Do, Miss Barnabetta," breathed Tess, eagerly.

"Oh! that will be lovely!" murmured Dot.

"Once upon a time a little brown toad—a very warty toad—lived in a little house he had scooped for himself in the dirt right under a rose tree. He was a very sensible, hard-workin' toad, only he grieved because he was so ugly.

"He never would have known he was so ugly, for he had no mirror in his house, if it hadn't been for the rose. But lookin' up at the buddin' rose, he saw how beautiful she was and knew that in contrast he was the very ugliest beast that moved upon the earth."

"The poor thing!" murmured Tess, the tender-hearted.

"He near about worshipped that rose," pursued Barnabetta, her own eyes brighter as the children followed her story breathlessly. "Every day he watched her unfold her petals more and more. He caught all the bugs and flies and ugly grubs he could to keep them from comin' at the rose and doin' her harm.

"Then came the mornin'," said Barnabetta, "when the rose was fully unfolded. The dew overnight had bejeweled each petal and when the first rays of the sun hurried to kiss her, the dewdrops sparkled like all manner of gems and precious stones.

"'Oh, see!' sighed the poor toad, 'how beautiful is the rose and how ugly I am.'

"But the rose heard him and she looked kindly down upon the poor toad. She knew how faithfully he had guarded her from the creepin' and flyin' things that would have spoiled her beauty.

"'Come here,' she said to the toad, bendin' down upon her stalk to see him better. And the toad hopped close beneath her. 'Come here,' said the rose, 'and I will make you, too, beautiful.'

"And then she called to the mornin' breeze, 'Shake me!' and the breeze did so—ever so gently—and all the sparklin', twinklin' precious gems of dewdrops shook off the rose and fell upon the toad in a shower.

"And at once," laughed Barnabetta, "the toad was covered with diamonds, and spangles, and glistenin' drops of dew in which the sun was reflected, till the toad appeared to be encased in an armor of silver, trimmed with jewels, and all the creatures in the garden cried:

"'Oh! how beautiful is the toad!'"

Agnes listened with delight to this fantasy from the trapeze performer. This gentle girl, telling pretty tales to Tess and Dot, was quite another person from "Barney" Scruggs, who had been tramping in boy's clothing with the old clown.

"She can't be wicked enough to have stolen that scrap-book," Agnes told herself, with increasing confidence. "Dear me! I wish I'd never found the old thing up garret."

The four Corner House girls went to church with Mrs. MacCall and Aunt Sarah. But Barnabetta would not go. She excused herself by saying that she did not wish to leave her father alone.

Sunday school followed the preaching service almost immediately; but as soon as this was over, Agnes hurried home. Ruth, with Tess and Dot, went around by the hospital to call on Mrs. Eland, the matron, and to enquire after Miss Pepperill.

They chanced to find the little gray lady sitting at her desk, and with certain yellowed old papers and letters, and several small books with ragged sheepskin covers, before her.

"These were Uncle Lemuel's," she explained to Ruth, touching the dog's-eared books. "His diaries. It does seem as though he loved to put down on paper all his miserly thoughts and accounts of his very meanest acts. He must have been a strange combination of business acumen and simple-mindedness."

"I wish for your sake, Mrs. Eland," Ruth said, "that he had kept to the very day of his death the riches he once accumulated."

"Oh! I wish so, too—for Teeny's sake," replied Mrs. Eland, referring to her unfortunate sister by the pet name she had called her in childhood.

"Are these the books and papers Mr. Bob Buckham brought you from the Quoharie poorhouse, where Mr. Aden died?"

"Yes. I have never read through the diaries. I only wanted to find an account of the five hundred dollars belonging to Mr. Buckham's father that myfather turned over to Uncle Lemuel.

"But here are notes of really vast sums. Uncle Lemuel must have really been quite beside himself long before he died. In one place he writes about drawing out of several banks sums aggregating over fifty thousand dollars.

"Think of it!" and Mrs. Eland sighed. "It was at the time of the panic. He speaks of being distrustful of banks. So he drew out all he had. But, of course, he did not have so much money as that. Fifty thousand dollars!"

"Perhaps he did have it," said Ruth.

"Then what became of it? He writes in one place of losing a hundred dollars in some transaction, and he goes on about it, in a raving way, as though it was every cent of money he ever owned," declared Mrs. Eland. "Oh, dear! What a terrible thing it must be to be a miser."

"But—but suppose he did have so much money at one time?"

"He dreamed it," laughed the hospital matron.

"You're not sure," ventured the Corner House girl.

"Then what became of it? I am sure he never gave it away," Mrs. Eland said, shaking her head. "And here, where he speaks of coming to live with your Uncle Peter Stower, in the very last year of his life, Uncle Lemuel says:

"'Peter Stower always was a fool. He'll give me bite and sup as long as I need. Let him believe me rich or poor as he pleases.'"

"Oh, dear me," sighed Ruth, "I always have felt bad because Uncle Peter turned him out and Mr. Aden wandered away to die at the Quoharie poorhouse. Your uncle couldn't have been in his right mind."

"Of course he wasn't," rejoined Mrs. Eland. "Why! it shows that here. On almost the last page of his diary—it was written after he left the old Corner House—he says:

"'I don't trust banks; but Peter Stower is too mean to be dishonest. My book is safe with him.'

"I suppose," the little gray lady said, "Uncle Lemuel had an idea of sending these diaries to your Uncle Peter to keep for him. I can't think of any other book he was referring to."

"A book?" murmured Ruth, quaveringly.

"Yes. And once before he speaks here—where is it?—of his diary, I suppose, as his 'beautiful book.' Ah! here it is: 'Have pasted all my Wash. & Pitts. R. R. B.'s in my beautiful book.' Now," and Mrs. Eland laughed, "what do you suppose 'Wash. & Pitts.' means?"

Ruth sprang up, trembling, and with clasped hands.

"Oh, Mrs. Eland!" she cried, "'Washington & Pittsburgh'—and he meant railroad bonds, of course! It must be! it must be!"

"Well—but—my dear!" said Mrs. Eland, amazed by Ruth's excitement. "Of course, Uncle Lemuel may have meant that. However, there are no bonds of any kind pasted into these books. I am sure of that," and she laughed again, but rather ruefully.

Ruth Kenway could not join in her laughter. She had made a tremendous discovery—and one that filled her with actual terror. She scarcely knew how she managed to excuse herself from the hospital matron's presence, and got out upon the street again with Tess and Dot.

CHAPTER XXI—"EVERYTHING AT SIXES AND SEVENS"

"I do declare," said Agnes Kenway, that very evening. "We don't seem like ourselves. The house doesn't seem like our house. And we're all at sixes and sevens! What ever is the matter with Ruthie?"

For the eldest Corner House girl had spoken crossly to Tess, and had fairly shaken Dot for leaving a chocolate-cream on a chair where she, Ruth, sat down upon it in her best dress, and finally she had flown out of the sitting room in tears and run up to bed.

"And Neale didn't stay to eat supper last night, and he hasn't been here to-day," grieved Tess.

"Here's all his Christmas presents," said Dot. "Don't you s'pose he wants them a-tall? Is Neale mad, too?"

"I'm afraid Ruthie is coming down with something—like Sammy Pinkney with the scarlet fever," Tess said, in a worried tone.

Agnes knew that it must be worry over the lost album and money that had got upon her older sister's nerves. But even she did not suspect the full measure of Ruth's trouble, for the latter had said nothing about the discovery in Lemuel Aden's old diary. But Agnes heartily wished she had never made that odd find in the garret.

She had not seen Barnabetta save at dinner time, and the clown had not left his room. Agnes was troubled about Barnabetta. The little girls found the trapeze artist a most delightful companion; but Barnabetta had scarcely a word to say to either of the older Corner House sisters.

As for Neale—Agnes Kenway could have cried about Neale. She and the white-haired boy had been the very best of friends.

"And I'm sure I didn't say anything to anger him. He needn't have got mad at me," was Agnes' thought. "Whatever he wanted in that closet last night—

"There! I won't believe it was Neale at all. Why should he want to steal anything here, when he could have had it for the asking?

"But who else could have gotten out of that porch door, past Tom Jonah, without being eaten up?" murmured poor Agnes. "Oh, dear me! how can I believe it of him?"

Really, everything was at sixes and at sevens. The week began badly. The two smallest Corner House girls seemed afflicted with a measure of the unhappiness that cloaked Ruth, Agnes and their guest, Barnabetta Scruggs.

Dot actually quarreled with Mabel Creamer! It came about in this wise:

After school on Monday the smallest Corner House girl had been to the store for Mrs. MacCall. Coming home, as she came past the Creamer cottage she heard Mrs. Creamer scolding Mabel.

"You bad, bad girl!" the unwise mother was saying to the sullen Mabel. "I should think your little brother would cry whenever you come near him. You don't deserve to have a dear, baby brother. Get out of my sight, you naughty child!"

When Mabel appeared at her gate to face the wondering Dot, she did not look heart-broken because Bubby had taken a sudden dislike to her.

"What ever is the matter, Mabel Creamer?" asked the smallest Corner House girl.

"Oh—nothin'. Only I just fixed that kid for once," declared Mabel, with impish satisfaction. "I don't believe they'll leave me to watch him all the time while Lyddy and Peg go off to a movin' pitcher show."

"Oh, my!" said the awe-struck Dot. "What ever did you do?"

"I'll tell you what I did, Dot Kenway," said Mabel, dropping her voice to a whisper. "Bubby wants to be played with all the time. You don't get a minute to call your soul your own," she added, quoting some of her elders.

"So, if he wanted to be amused all so fine, I amused him. I smeared molasses on his fingers and then I gave him a feather out of the pillow. Oh, he was amused! He was trying to pick that feather off his fingers for half an hour, and was just as still as still! It might ha' lasted longer, too, only he got mad with the feather, and bawled."

Dot did not know whether to laugh at, or be horrified by, such depravity as this. But she was glad that Mabel was free to go home with her at this time, for Tess had been kept after school.

"We've got four of just the cunningest kittens," Dot said, to her visitor. "Of course, they are really Almira's. Santa Claus got them for her. But wecall them ours."

"My! isn't that fine?" cried Mabel. "We've got two cats, but they're lazy old things. They never have any kittens. We call them Paul and Timothy."

Almira's young family still nested upon Unc' Rufus' old coat in the woodshed. Dot put two in her apron to bring them out on the porch where the cunning little things could be seen. But when Mabel grabbed up the other two there was a good deal of noise attending the operation.

"Oh, Mabel! don't hurt them," cried Dot.

"I'm not hurting them," responded Mabel, sharply. "I'm carrying them just as careful as I can by their stems."

"Oh, dear—don't!" shrieked Dot, quite horrified. "Them's their tails, Mabel Creamer."

"Huh! what else are they for, I'd like to know?" propounded the visitor. "A cat's tail is made for it to be grabbed by."

"You—you——You're cruel, Mabel Creamer!" gasped Dot. "Put them down!"

She tumbled the two staggering kittens out of her own lap and ran to rescue the poor, squalling mites in Mabel's hands. Mabel was not a child to be driven in any case. There was a struggle. Dot rescued the two little mites, but Mabel slapped the little Corner House girl's cheek twice—and her hand left its mark.

"You're a nasty little thing, Dot Kenway!" scolded Mabel, marching down the steps and out at the gate. "I never did like you much, and I just hateyou, now."

Dot sat down, sobbing, on the step, and nursed the bruised cheek. The four little kittens squirmed all over her lap and tumbled about like drunken caterpillars—and that helped some. For soon the tears were dried and Dot began to laugh at their antics. Just the same, Mabel's blow had left a bruise upon the smallest Corner House girl's heart which she long remembered.

Tess had had a rather hard day, too. Of course, there was a new teacher ruling over the eighth grade; and strict as Miss Pepperill had been, even Sammy Pinkney would have been glad to "swap back" for the red-haired teacher, after a session's experience with Miss Grimsby.

Miss Grimsby was young, but she looked a lot older than most of the other teachers. She wore her sleek, black hair brushed straight back from a high, blue-veined forehead. She wore enormous, shell-bowed spectacles.

Miss Grimsby was what is known as a substitute teacher. She had brought to her work in the eighth grade the very newest ideas about teaching taught in the normal schools. She knew all about her textbooks, and how to teach the studies allotted her; but she did not know the first living thing about those small animals known as boys and girls.

She was fond of standing up before the class and giving little lectures upon a multitude of subjects. This method of teaching was much approved by the faculty of the normal college from which Miss Grimsby had just graduated.

Poor Jakey Gerlach had already come into conflict with the new teacher, and once having decided that Jakey was a "bad" boy, Miss Grimsby saw him only in that peculiar light, no matter what he did.

"Children," said she, on one occasion, "you should be able to do anything equally well with either hand. That is called 'being ambidextrous.' See! I write with either hand, like this," and she illustrated with chalk upon the blackboard.

"With a little practice you will find it just as easy to do anything with one hand as it is with the other. Will you try? Jakey Gerlach! What are you squirming there for in that disgraceful manner?"

"I—I—please, Teacher," stammered Jakey, "I was only trying to put mine left hand in mine right-hand trousers' pocket."

And Jakey remained after school for this. He was not alone in his punishment. More than half the eighth grade began to report late at their homes nowadays.

On this special "blue Monday," Tess Kenway was one of the unfortunates. Without being a goody-goody girl, Tess had a remarkable record for deportment. It hurt her cruelly to be told to remain with the other culprits on this occasion.

Nor did she think she deserved the punishment. It came about through her trying to help Etta Spears, who sat across the aisle from Tess.

Etta got up to recite and dropped her slate pencil. When the next girl, Julia Bowen, was called to arise, she would be sure to put her foot upon the pencil and break it. So Tess leaned from her seat to rescue the pencil.

"What are you doing—crawling on the floor there—Theresa?" demanded Miss Grimsby, sharply.

"I—I was reaching for this pencil, please, Teacher," said Tess, holding up her prize.

"Bring it here instantly! If you can't keep your pencils in their proper place in your desk, you must lose them."

"Oh, but please, Miss Grimsby! It isn't my pencil," gasped Tess.

"Then, what are you doing with it?" demanded the teacher, severely.

"Oh, Teacher!" almost sobbed Tess.

"Bring that pencil here!"

"But it is Etta's!" Tess, in desperation, cried.

"How came it on the floor?"

"She dropped it, Teacher."

"Bring it here. Etta will go without her pencil for a day. You, Theresa, will remain after school for interfering with the pencil and for interrupting the class.

"Next girl! Julia Bowen! Rise!"

So Tess was not at home when Mabel Creamer slapped Dot and broke the truce that had endured for a long time between the Creamer cottage and the old Corner House.

Of course, Dot told her all about it. Tess was the gentlest child imaginable, but that Dot should have been struck, stirred the older sister "all up."

"The awful thing!" she gasped. "Why—why didn't you call Ruthie—or Aggie?"

"Why—ee!" said Dot, slowly. "What good would that do, Tessie? They couldn't put the slap back. My face would have ached just the same."

"Never mind, dear," crooned Tess. "I'll give you my best pencil. I don't much care for pencils any more, anyway."

Ruth had been to the bank again at noon. She showed the old banknote to the cashier, Mr. Crouch being out. The cashier said the bill was perfectly good.

"And that settles it," she said, wearily, to Agnes, on their way home from school. "If one bill is good the others must be."

"Oh! I can't believe it!" murmured Agnes. "Fifty thousand dollars in cash!"

"And as much more in unregistered railroad bonds. They were perfectly good, too—and there must be a lot of dividends due upon them. Oh, a fortune indeed!" groaned Ruth, in conclusion.

"I can't believe it," repeated her astonished sister.

"I can believe it—very easily," Ruth retorted. It was on the tip of her tongue to tell Agnes that all that fortune they had lost belonged to Mrs. Eland and Miss Pepperill. But Agnes said:

"But Neale could not possibly have known it was good."

"Oh! Neale!" exclaimed Ruth, exasperated.

"You don't really believe he would do anything wrong, do you, Ruthie?" queried Agnes, pleadingly.

"He did enough wrong when he carried that book away with him to Tiverton."

"But I let him have the book," Agnes confessed.

"He had no right to go off with it," the other said stubbornly. "And when he brought it back, why did he throw it down there on the porch in that careless manner?"

"Of course he didn't know the money was good," Agnes repeated, trying to bolster up her own shaking faith in Neale O'Neil.

For a very unhappy thought had come into Agnes' mind. Ruth had been so certain that the money and the bonds were good that she might have convinced

Neale that evening, when he had come home from Tiverton. Agnes was quite sure he had not considered the printed banking paper worth anything before that time. Had he found a chance to take the book out of the bag and hide it after he had flung himself in anger out of the sitting room?

"I don't know how he could have done it," groaned Agnes, to herself. "But why did he come back again that night, if it wasn't for the album?"

She had to admit that Neale must have been the midnight visitor to the dining room. There was no other explanation of that incident.

Neale had not been to church on Sunday, but she had seen him at school on this day, for he was in her grade; but he had not spoken to her or even looked at her.

Agnes was hurt to the quick by this. She felt that Ruth had been unkind to Neale; but on her part she was sure she was guilty of no unfriendliness.

"He needn't spit it out on me," was the way Agnes inelegantly expressed it. "And why did he want to come over here and play burglar Saturday night? And goodness! what did he want in that closet in the dining room chimney?"

"He surely wouldn't want Aunt Sarah's peppermints," she giggled. "And what else is there in that cupboard?"

The thought sent Agnes marching into the dining room to look at the locked door. And there stood Barnabetta Scruggs!

Barnabetta was at the door of the closet in the chimney. She did not appear to hear Agnes come into the room. She was closely examining the lock on the closet door.

"What under the sun is she after?" thought Agnes. "What's that in her hand? A pair of shears?"

Barnabetta raised the shears just as though she contemplated trying to pick the lock with them. She laid hold upon the knob and shook the door.

"For pity's sake, Barnabetta!" exclaimed Agnes. "What do you want there?"

The circus girl jumped and actually screamed. Her thin face flushed and then paled. Her eyes flashed.

"I might ha' known 'twas you—always snoopin' around!" snarled Barnabetta.

"Why—why—"

"Can't I look at that old lock if I want to? I'm not hurtin' it."

"And I'm pretty sure you can't unlock it with those shears," returned the wondering Agnes.

"Who's trying to unlock it?" snapped Barnabetta.

"You were."

"Weren't, neither!" declared the circus girl, throwing down the shears. "Leastways, not for myself," she added.

"I'd like to know what it is you want out of that closet—what anybody wants there," Agnes said, wonderingly.

"Your auntie wants some more peppermints," said Barnabetta, boldly. "She couldn't unlock it with the key. I didn't know but the lock could be picked."

"Where's the key?" asked Agnes, swiftly.

"Your auntie took it away with her again."

Agnes stared at her in amazement. She believed Barnabetta must be telling an untruth. "I'm going to find out what's in that closet—that's what I am going to do," she declared.

She marched out of the room. She heard Barnabetta laugh unpleasantly as she closed the door. Agnes went up to Aunt Sarah's room.

"Aunt Sarah," Agnes said earnestly, "won't you let me have the key of the dining room closet? I want to get something out of it."

"Good Land of Liberty!" exclaimed Aunt Sarah, with asperity. "You're welcome to that old key, I'm sure. I dunno why I brought it up here again. Ye can't unlock it, gal. I declare! I was an old silly to lock the door the other night. Now the lock's fouled and ye can't turn the key neither-which-way!"

She took the big brass key out of her bag and handed it to the amazed Agnes. Agnes was amazed because she had discovered that Barnabetta had told the truth about it!

CHAPTER XXII—BARNABETTA CONFESSES

When Agnes reached the dining room again, the circus girl was gone. She tried the key in the lock of the cupboard door. Just as Aunt Sarah Maltby said, it would not turn. Something had fouled the lock.

"I do declare!" thought the troubled and perplexed Agnes. "This is the strangest thing. I never did want to get into this old cupboard before; but I feel now as though I'd just got to.

"There surely is something in it besides Aunt Sarah's peppermints. Barnabetta told the truth about Aunt Sarah; but she had a personal reason for wanting to open the door, too. I'm certain of that. Dear me! What is this mystery? I want to know."

She did not see how she could pick the lock of the closet door herself. She knew nothing about such work. Agnes wished Neale were friendly with them so that she could ask him.

And then immediately she was smitten with the thought that Neale O'Neil was another person who seemed curious about what was in the closet.

"Oh, dear me!" murmured Agnes. "What a terrible mix-up this is. What ever shall I do about it?"

Her greatest desire, next to being friends with Neale O'Neil again, was to take Ruth into her confidence about her adventure Saturday night with the mysterious burglar. But because suspicion must point directly to Neale, she could not bring herself to talk it over with her sister.

And Ruth, fearing to take anybody into her confidence regarding the real ownership of the lost treasure, was passing through a sea of troubled waters without even Agnes to confess to. The oldest Corner House girl was, at this very moment, sitting in her room trying to compose a letter to Mr. Howbridge that should reveal the whole story. She supposed the lawyer's clerk would know how to reach him, for Ruth had forgotten that Tiverton was the name of the town to which Mr. Howbridge had been called by his brother's illness.

With her pen poised over the page of her letter she wondered how she should word her confession to Mr. Howbridge. For Ruth felt that she, herself, was much to blame for the final loss of the treasure.

Although she blamed Neale to her sister, in her heart Ruth knew that had she been wiser in the first place, all this mystery and difficulty following the odd find in the Corner House garret, would never have arisen.

If she had done one of two things, right then and there, she saw now that the album would never have gone out of her custody.

She should either have taken Agnes and Neale into her confidence and shown them the book, and told them she had extracted one of the ten dollar bills to show to Mr. Crouch at the bank; or she should have locked the old album away in a perfectly safe place until the value of the paper could be determined.

It is only human nature to look for some scapegoat for our sins. Knowing herself to have neglected proper precautions, it was quite natural that Ruth should blame Neale. But now she blamed herself. Poor Mrs. Eland! And poor Miss Pepperill! In her heart of hearts Ruth had longed to do something worth while to help the two unfortunate ladies. And all the time a fortune belonging to them was hid away in the garret of the old Corner House.

"Oh, dear me!" she moaned, sitting over her unfinished letter. "Why should they be punished for my neglect? It is not fair!"

She heard a door open, and then voices. The sound was right on this floor.

"I tell you we've got to go, Pop. Well slip out of the side door and nobody will notice us. It's gettin' dark," said an anxious young voice.

"I don't see why we got to go, Barney," responded a querulous voice.

"I tell you we can't stay here another minute. Seems to me I shall die if we do!"

Ruth sprang up and ran softly to the door of her room. Asa Scruggs' complaining voice retorted:

"I don't know what's got inter ye, Barney. You know I can't hobble a block. These folks is mighty kind. We ain't got a right to treat 'em so."

"We're treatin' 'em better by goin' away than by stayin'," declared the other voice. "I tell you, Pop, we've got to go!"

Ruth opened her door. A lithe, boyish figure was aiding the limping clown along the passage toward the back stairway. But the face the strange figure turned to Ruth was that of Barnabetta Scruggs.

"Why! Why, Barnabetta!" gasped the Corner House girl in vast amazement.

Barnabetta was dumb. The weak mouth of the old circus clown trembled, and his eyes blinked, as he stood there on one foot, and stared, speechless, at their hostess.

"Why, Barnabetta!" cried Ruth again. "What ever is the matter?"

"We're goin'," said the circus girl, sullenly.

"Going where?"

"Well! we're not goin' to stay here," said Barnabetta.

"Why, Barnabetta! Why not?"

"We're not—that's all," ejaculated the trapeze artist.

"But I am sure your father isn't fit to leave the house," Ruth said. "Surely, you know you are welcome to remain till he is quite well."

"We've got no business here. We never ought to've come," said Barnabetta.

"Why not? You make us no trouble. I am sure you have been treated kindly."

"What for?" snapped Barnabetta. "You folks have got no call to treat us kind. We're nothin' to you."

"Oh, Barnabetta! I thought we were friends," the Corner House girl said, really grieved by this. "I would not keep you a moment longer than you wish to stay; but I hope you understand that you and Mr. Scruggs are perfectly welcome here.

"And I don't want you to go away in those boy's clothes, Barnabetta. You tell me your other clothing is all in your trunk at the express office in Tiverton. Why not send for it? But the frock and other things I let you have, I meant for you to keep."

"I don't want 'em," said Barnabetta, ungratefully. "If we've got to tramp it, I can't be bothered with skirts."

"But my dear!" cried Ruth, desperately, "your father can't walk. Of course he can't!"

"We've got to get down South where we can get a job with some tent show," Barnabetta declared, deaf to Ruth's objections.

"Mr. Scruggs! You know you can't get there," Ruth cried. "And if you really must go, Barnabetta—"

"I can get a job, anyway," said the girl.

"Then let me help you on your way. Where do you want to go? Maybe I can pay your fare and you can pay me back when—when you have luck again."

"Hear that, Barney?" gasped Asa Scruggs. "She's right. I can't walk yet."

"I'm not goin' to take money from these girls!"

"Only as a loan?" begged Ruth.

"Aw—we'll never get so we could pay you back," groaned Barnabetta, hopelessly. "We're in bad, and that's all there is to it."

Mr. Scruggs leaned against the wall and looked at Ruth timidly. Evidently he had been all through the argument with his stubborn daughter already.

"I cannot understand you, Barnabetta," said Ruth, sadly. "For your father's sake—at least, let him stay with us till his ankle is better."

"He can stay," said Barnabetta, quickly. "If he will."

"We've never been separated yet, miss," Asa Scruggs said to Ruth, excusingly. "Not since her mother left her to me—a baby in arms.

"Barnabetta was brought up in the circus. I cradled her in my make-up tray, and she slept there, or sucked at her bottle, when I was out in the ring doin' my turn as a joey.

"She ain't had much experience outside the big top. She couldn't be sure of gettin' a safe job—only a young gal like her—lest I was with her."

"Why!" exclaimed Ruth, more cheerfully. "Let her wait here—with you—Mr. Scruggs. Maybe we can find her a job right here in Milton, until your ankle is well enough for you to travel."

"Huh!" snorted Barnabetta. "Who wants a lady acrobat, I'd like to know, in this 'hick' burg?"

"But, can't you do anything else, Barnabetta?" asked Ruth, more eagerly. "Couldn't you 'tend counter in a candy store like June Wildwood? Or maybe we could get you a chance in the Five and Ten Cent Store. Oh! as soon as Mr. Howbridge gets home, I am sure he can help us."

"We're not a-goin' to stay," interrupted Barnabetta, still bitterly antagonistic to every suggestion of the Corner House girl. "Come on, Pop."

"Aw, Barney! Listen to reason," begged the clown.

"We haven't got a right to," gasped Barnabetta. "I tell you these girls will want to put us in jail."

"What for?" demanded Ruth, wonderingly.

"Well me in jail, then. Pop hasn't done anything.'"

"But, for pity's sake, what for?"

"If you knew what I was—what I did—"

"What did you do, Barnabetta?" queried Ruth, with some excitement.

"I—I stole that old book you're huntin' for. It was me took it out of Neale Sorber's bag. That's what!"

The confession burst from Barnabetta wildly.

"I knew there was money in it. I saw it when he was up to the winter quarters of the circus at Tiverton. That other girl knew I saw it. Hasn't she told you?"

"Who—Aggie?" asked the amazed Ruth.

"Yes. She knows what I am—a thief!"

"No! Oh, no, Barnabetta! Don't call yourself that. And Agnes never said a word to me against you. Agnes likes you."

"I don't see how she can. She knew I wanted to steal the book. She must have guessed I got it out of Neale's bag Saturday night. And I guess now she knows what I did with it."

"Oh, Barnabetta! What did you do with it?" cried Ruth, forgetting everything else but the sudden hope that the album might be recovered.

"I put it in the bottom of that closet downstairs in the dinin' room," confessed Barnabetta, bursting into tears. "And your auntie locked the door and I couldn't get at it again. And now she can't unlock it.

"I—I was hopin' I could get the book and give it back to you—leave it somewhere where you'd be sure to see it. I was ashamed of what I'd done. I wouldn't touch a dollar of that money in it—not now, after you'd been so awful nice to me and Pop. And—and—"

But here Ruth put both arms around her and stopped her lips with a kiss.

"Oh, Barnabetta! Don't say another word!" she cried. "You have made me the happiest girl in all the world to-day!"

Barnabetta stared at her, open-mouthed and wide-eyed.

"What's that you're sayin', Miss Ruth?" asked the clown.

"Why, don't you see?" cried Ruth, laughing and sobbing together. "I thought the book was really lost—that we'd never recover it. And I've just discovered that all that money and those bonds in it belong to our dear friend, Mrs. Eland, and her sister, who is in the hospital. Oh! and they need the money so badly!

"Just think! it is a fortune. There's fifty thousand dollars in money besides the bonds. And I took one of the notes to the bank and found out for sure that the money is good.

"Oh, dear me!" cried Ruth, in conclusion, sobbing and laughing together until she hiccoughed. "Oh, dear me! I never was so delighted by anything in my life—not even when we came here to live at the old Corner House!"

"But—but—isn't the money yours, Ruth?" asked Barnabetta. "Doesn't it belong to you Corner House girls?"

"Oh, no. It was money left by Mr. Lemuel Aden when he died. I am sure of that. And Mrs. Eland and Miss Pepperill are his nieces."

"Then it doesn't mean anything to you if the money is found?" gasped the circus girl.

"Of course it means something to me—to us all. Of course it does, Barnabetta. I never can thank you enough for telling me—"

"But I stole it first and put it there," said Barnabetta.

"Never mind! Don't worry about that. Let us run down and get the book out of the closet. And don't dare leave this house, either of you!" she commanded, running down the back stairs.

Barnabetta helped her father back to his room. Then she went down the front flight and met the excited Ruth and the quite amazed Agnes in the dining room. Ruth had the heavy kitchen poker.

"What under the sun are you going to do with that poker, Ruth Kenway?" demanded Agnes.

"Oh, Aggie! Think of it! That old album is locked in that closet."

"Well! didn't I just begin to believe so myself?" ejaculated the second Corner House girl.

Ruth waited for no further explanation. She pressed the heavy poker into the aperture between the lock of the door and the striker, pushing as hard as she could, and then used the strong poker as a prize. The door creaked.

"You'll break it!" gasped Agnes.

"That's what I mean to do. We can't unlock it," said Ruth, with determination.

The next moment, with a splintering of wood, the lock gave and the door swung open. Ruth flung down the poker and dived into the bottom of the closet.

Up she came with her prize. Unmistakably it was the album Agnes had found in the garret.

"Hurrah!" shouted Agnes. "Oh, dear! I'm so glad—"

But Ruth uttered a cry of despair. She had brought the old volume to the table and opened it. The yellowed and paste-stained pages were bare!

Swiftly she fluttered the leaves from the front to the back cover. Not a bond, not a banknote, was left in the book. Everything of value had been removed, and the girls, horror-stricken, realized that the treasure was as far from their custody as ever.

CHAPTER XXIII—WHO WAS THE ROBBER?

That was a terrible moment in the lives of the two older Corner House girls.

Terrible for Ruth, because she saw crushed thus unexpectedly her desire to make Mrs. Eland and her sister happy and comfortable for life. Terrible for Agnes, because she could think of nobody but Neale O'Neil who could have got at the album and abstracted the money and bonds.

"Oh, dear! oh, dear! oh, dear!" wailed Agnes, and threw herself into a chair, despairingly.

Ruth was pallid. Barnabetta Scruggs stared at the two Corner House girls with horrified, wide-open eyes.

"Now—now," the circus girl muttered, "you girls won't ever believe a word I say!"

"Why not, Barnabetta?" asked Agnes.

"I told your sister I put that album in the closet—and I did. But I didn't take even one banknote out of the book!"

"I believe you, Barnabetta," Ruth said faintly. "But—but who is the robber?"

"I was enough of a thief to take the book out of Neale's bag," said the circus girl. "But I didn't even look into it. I didn't have time."

"How did you come to do it?" asked Agnes, curiously.

"I heard Neale when he came here Saturday night. Of course, I knew 'twas him by his voice and what you girls said. And I heard there was some kind of a row."

"There was," sighed Agnes.

"I came down and listened at the door of that other room where you girls and Neale were talkin'. I heard him say the book was in his bag on the porch, and I knew that bag didn't have any lock to it."

"Of course," groaned Ruth.

"I was goin' to get it before he came out; but he flung open the sittin' room door so quick he pretty near caught me. I crouched down in the corner at the foot of the stairs and if he hadn't been so mad," said Barnabetta, "he must have seen me.

"But he didn't, and when he was gone I went outside and got the book. You girls were still in the sittin' room; but I heard somebody up in the back hall and I was afraid to go upstairs, either by the back or the front flight.

"So I slipped into the dinin' room and there was little Dottie. I kept the book behind me and didn't know what to do with it. But Dottie ran out of the room and I plumped it into that closet and shut the door quick," finished Barnabetta.

"And is that all?" Ruth said, very much disappointed.

"I—I never saw the book again till just now."

"Oh!" began Agnes, when the circus girl interrupted her, jerkily.

"I—I tried to see it. I was goin' to steal the money—or, some of it, anyway. I know you'll think me awful. But—but we were so hard up, and all—just the same, I couldn't get into the closet again.

"I staid awake Saturday night, and when I thought everybody was abed and the house was still, I came down here in this boy's suit—"

"Oh!" cried Agnes again—and this time in a much relieved tone. But Barnabetta did not notice.

"Your aunt came down with her candle for those peppermints before I could get at the book."

"But what did you do then?" asked the eager and curious Agnes.

"I was just about crazy," admitted the circus girl. "I thought I'd done that sin of stealin' the book and it had done us no good. I wanted to run away right then and there—I'd have left poor Pop behind.

"But when I got the porch door out there ready to open, I heard your old dog snuffin' outside, and it scared me pretty near to death. I knew he wouldn't let me out—and I was afraid he'd bite me if I let him in.

"So I ran upstairs and shut myself into that room again. And I didn't dare come out till mornin'."

"Oh, thank goodness!" gasped Agnes, under her breath. "It wasn't Neale O'Neil!"

But this did not explain the mystery of the disappearance of the treasure trove that had been found in the Corner House garret. The Kenway girls were sure that Barnabetta Scruggs had told them the truth. She was not to blame for the actual robbery.

"And that must have occurred some time before you came down to look for the book Saturday night, Barnabetta," Ruth said. "What time was it?"

"Oh, about midnight."

"Then the robber got at the book some time in the hour between half past ten and half past eleven. Mrs. MacCall did not retire until half past ten, that is sure."

"But how did he get in, and how did he get out, and who, for pity's sake, is he?" cried Agnes.

Ruth shook her head. She might have said that her acquaintance among burglars was just as limited as Agnes' own.

Only, this was no occasion for humor. The loss of a treasure amounting, possibly, to a hundred thousand dollars was no subject for raillery.

"What will Mr. Howbridge say!" groaned Ruth.

"Oh, dear me! Let's not worry about what he says!" cried Agnes. "It's nothing to him. Think of it! We are the losers of all that money."

"No," Ruth said quickly.

"Why not? What do you mean?" demanded her sister.

"It is a great loss, an irreparable loss, to the real owners of the fortune."

"Well, who are they?" demanded Agnes. "We don't know them. I suppose the courts would have to decide. But I guess a part of the money, anyway, would come to us. Enough to buy an automobile."

"No," repeated Ruth, shaking her head.

"Why not?" cried her sister. "Of course it's ours!"

"That's what I say. But your sister wants to give it all away," said Barnabetta.

"Give it all away!" cried Agnes.

"It isn't ours—or, it wasn't ours—to give," Ruth declared.

"I should say not!" ejaculated the puzzled Agnes.

"But I do know whom it belonged to," said Ruth, quietly.

"Not Aunt Sarah?" gasped Agnes.

"No. Nobody at all here. It was hidden in our garret by Lemuel Aden when he was here the last time to see Uncle Peter."

"Goodness me!" cried Agnes. "Lemuel Aden? That wicked old miser?"

"Yes."

"But how do you know, Ruth Kenway? I thought he died in a poorhouse?"

"He did. That was like the miser he was."

"But, if he's dead—?" But Agnes did not follow the idea to its conclusion.

"Why, don't you see," Ruth hastened to say. "The money belongs to Mr. Aden's nieces—Mrs. Eland and Miss Pepperill. And they need it so!"

"Oh, my goodness! so it does!"

"And we have lost it!" finished Ruth, in despair.

"Well! they can't blame us," Agnes said, swift to be upon the defensive.

"But I blame myself. I should have taken more care of the book, in the first place."

"Then you don't blame Neale?" demanded Agnes, quickly.

"He's to blame for carrying the book off without saying anything about it to us," said Ruth. "But I am mainly at fault."

"No," said Barnabetta suddenly. "I'm to blame. If I had left the book in the bag on the porch, you girls would have found it all right, and the money would not have been stolen."

"I don't see how you make that out," Agnes said. "If the robber found the book in that closet where you hid it, why couldn't he have found it anywhere else in the house?"

"Perhaps not if I had locked it in the silver safe in the pantry," Ruth said slowly.

"Oh, well! what does it matter who's at fault?" Agnes demanded, impatiently. "The money's gone."

"Yes, it's gone," repeated her sister. "And poor Mrs. Eland and Miss Pepperill, who need it so much, will never see it."

"You girls worry a lot over other folks' troubles," said Barnabetta. "And those women you tell about don't even know that their grandfather left the money, do they?"

"Their uncle," corrected Ruth.

"Of course not," said Agnes, in reply to Barnabetta, and quite subdued now by Ruth's revelation regarding the probable owners of the fortune. "But, you see, Barnabetta, they are our friends; and we wanted very much to help them, anyway."

"And it did seem as though Providence must have sent us to that corner of the garret that evening, just so Agnes should find the old album," added Ruth.

"But I wish I hadn't found it!" wailed Agnes, suddenly. "Just see the trouble we're in."

"Then I guess 'twasn't providential your goin' there, was it?" demanded Barnabetta.

"We can't say that," responded Ruth, thoughtfully.

"You Corner House girls are the greatest!" burst out the trapeze performer. "I never saw anybody like you! Do you spend all your time tryin' to help other folks?"

"Why—we help when we can and where we can," Ruth said.

"It's lots of fun, too," put in Agnes. "It's nice to make friends."

"Why—I believe it must be," sighed Barnabetta. "But I never thought of it—just so. I never saw folks like you Corner House girls before. That's what made me feel so mean when I had robbed you."

"Oh, don't let's talk any more about that," Ruth said, with her old kindness of tone and manner. "We'll forget it."

But Barnabetta said, seriously: "I never can. Don't think it! I'm goin' to remember it all the days of my life. And I know it's my fault that you've lost all the money."

Ruth returned the poker to its place, and Agnes swept up the chips of wood and the bits of the broken lock. Ruth carefully put away the big old book Agnes had found in the garret.

"Locking the barn after the horse is stolen," commented Agnes.

Ruth felt that she could not finish that letter to Mr. Howbridge. There was no haste about it. She could wait to tell him all about the catastrophe when he returned to Milton. Advice now was of no value to her. The fortune was gone. Indeed, she shrank from talking about it any more. Talk would not bring the treasure back, that was sure.

She had not Agnes' overpowering curiosity. There was a sort of dumb ache at Ruth's heart, and she sighed whenever she remembered poor Mrs. Eland and her sister.

If Dr. Forsyth was to be believed, a long, long rest was Miss Pepperill's only cure. News from the State Hospital had assured the friends of the unfortunate school teacher that she would soon be at liberty.

But she might then lapse into a morose and unfortunate state of mind, unless she could rest, have a surcease of worry, and a change of scene. How could poor Mrs. Eland leave her position to care for her sister? And how could either of them go away for a year or two to rest, with their small means?

It was, indeed, a very unfortunate condition of affairs. That the hospital matron knew nothing as yet about the fortune which should be her own and her sister's, made it no better in Ruth's opinion.

The more volatile Agnes could not be expected to feel so deeply the misfortune that had overtaken them. Besides, Agnes had one certain reason for being put in a happier frame of mind by the discovery they had just made.

The cloud of suspicion that had been raised in her thoughts by circumstantial evidence, no longer rested upon Neale O'Neil. If Neale would only "get over his mad fit," as Agnes expressed it, she thought she would be quite happy once more.

For never having possessed a hundred thousand dollars in fact, Agnes Kenway was not likely to weep much over its loss. The vast sum of money had really been nothing tangible to her.

Only for an hour or so after Ruth had been to the bank the second time and made sure that the money in the old album was legal tender, had Agnes really been convinced of its value. Then her thought had flown immediately to the possibility of their buying the long-wished-for automobile.

But the tempting possibility had no more than risen above the horizon of her mind than it had been eclipsed by the horrid discovery that a robber had relieved them of the treasure trove.

"So, that's all there is to that!" sighed Agnes to herself. "I guess the Corner House family won't ride in a car yet awhile."

When Ruth had spoken about Mrs. Eland and her sister, however, saying that the money really belonged to them, this thought finally gained a place in Agnes' mind, too. She was not at all a selfish girl, and she began to think that perhaps an automobile would not have been forthcoming after all.

"Goodness! what a little beast I am," she told herself in secret. "To think only of our own pleasure. Maybe, if the money hadn't been lost, Mrs. Eland would have given us enough out of it to buy the car. But just see what good could have come to poor Miss Pepperill and Mrs. Eland if the money had reached their hands.

"Mercy me!" pursued the next-to-the-oldest Corner House girl. "If I ever find a battered ten cent piece again, I'll believe it's good until it's proved to be lead. Just think! If I'd only had faith in that money in the old book being good, I'd have shouted loud enough to wake up the whole household, and surely somebody—Mrs. MacCall, or Ruth—would have kept me from letting poor Neale take the book away.

"Poor Neale!" she sighed again. "It wasn't his fault. He didn't believe that paper was any good—and those bonds. Of course he didn't. I—I wonder if he showed the bonds and money to anybody at all?"

This thought was rather a startling one. Her boy friend had taken the old album away from the Corner House in the first place with the avowed purpose of showing the bonds to somebody who would know about such things.

Of course, he did not show them to Mr. Con Murphy, the cobbler. And it did not seem as though he had had time on Christmas morning to show the book to anybody else before he went to Tiverton.

Nor would he have taken the book away if he had been decided, one way or the other, about the bonds and money. Had he shown them to any person while in Tiverton?

If so, Agnes suddenly wished to know who that person was. If Barnabetta Scruggs could get into Neale's room at the winter quarters of Twomley & Sorber's Herculean Circus and Menagerie, and could take a peep at the contents of the big book the boy carried in his bag, why could not some other— and some more evil-disposed person—have done the same?

Ruth had suggested it. She had said that a robber might have followed Neale O'Neil all the way from the circus and stolen the book off the porch of the old Corner House.

The same possibility held good regarding the removal of the money and the bonds from the book after Barnabetta had hidden it in the dining room closet. At that very moment the robber might have been in the house and seen what Barnabetta did with the book.

Of course, that was the explanation! Some hanger-on of the circus had followed Neale home to rob him—and had succeeded.

But, beyond that thought, and carrying the idea to its logical conclusion, Agnes pondered that Neale might have noticed that he was followed to Milton, and might know who the person was.

With Neale to suggest the identity of this robber, it might be possible to secure his person and recover the money. That idea no sooner took possession of Agnes Kenway's mind than she started up, ready and eager to do something to prove the thought correct.

"And I'll see Neale first of all. It all lies with him," she said aloud. "He's got to help us. I don't care if he is mad. He's just got to get over his mad and tell us how we shall go about finding the robber!"

CHAPTER XXIV—NEALE O'NEIL FLINGS A BOMB

Agnes came to her decision to interview Neale O'Neil just before the family dinner hour. She had to wait until after the meal before putting it into execution.

Ordinarily Neale would have been over at the old Corner House soon after seven o'clock with his books, ready to join the girls at their studies in the sitting room. He was not to be expected now, however. Only the little girls mentioned Neale's absence.

"I guess something has happened since Neale came home from the circus," Dot observed. "He don't seem to like us any more."

"I'm sure we've done nothing to him," said Tess, quite troubled. "But, anyway, you can't ever tell anything about boys—what they'll do. Can you, Ruthie?"

"There spoke the oracle," giggled Agnes.

"Tess is a budding suffragette," commented Mrs. MacCall.

"Oh, my! You sure won't be one of those awful suffering-etts when you grow up, will you, Tessie?" cried the horror-stricken Dot.

"Goodness! Suffragette, Dot!" admonished her sister. "But—but I guess I don't want to be one. They say Miss Grimsby is one and I'm sure I don't want to be anything she is."

"Is she very—very awful?" asked Dot, pityingly, yet with curiosity.

"She is awfully hard to get along with," admitted Tess. "Sometimes Miss Pepperill was cross; but Miss Grimsby is mad all the time."

"I—I wish they'd take Mabel Creamer into your room and let you take her place in mine," Dot said, feeling that her enemy next door should be put under the eye of just such a stern teacher as Miss Grimsby.

"I s'pose she'll make faces at me to-morrow," pursued Dot, with a sigh. "And she can make awful faces, you know she can, Tessie."

"Well, faces won't ever hurt you," the other sister said, philosophically.

"No-o," rejoined Dot. "Not really, of course. But," she confessed, "it makes you want to make faces, too. And I can't wriggle my face all up like Mabel Creamer can!"

Now, clothed in a proper frock again, Barnabetta Scruggs made one at the dinner table. She was subdued and rather silent; but as always she was kind to the children, beside whom she sat; and she was really grateful now to Ruth.

Despite her rough exterior, Barnabetta was kind at heart. She had only been hiding her good qualities from Ruth and Agnes because she knew in her heart that she meant to injure them. Now that she had confessed her wrong doing, her hardness of manner and foolish pride were all melted down. And nobody could long resist the sweetness of Ruth and the jollity of Agnes.

The latter slipped away right after dinner, leaving the little girls listening to one of Barnabetta's fairy stories—this time about The Horse That Made a House for the Birds.

"That circus girl is a good deal like a singed cat," remarked Mrs. MacCall in the kitchen. "I'm free to confess I didn't think much of her at first. You and Ruth do pick up some crooked sticks." She spoke to Agnes who was preparing to go out.

"But I watched her with the little ones and—bless her heart!—she's a real little woman! Working in a circus all her life hasn't spoiled her; but it isn't a business that I'd want a daughter of mine to follow.

"And there isn't a mite of harm in that Asa Scruggs," added the housekeeper. "Only I never did see such a melancholy looking man. And he a clown!"

Agnes was thinking how strange it was she should have met Barnabetta and her father in the woods and brought them home, when they had come from the Twomley & Sorber Circus, and knew Neale O'Neil. And what would Neale say when he learned that the clown and his daughter were at the old Corner House?

Agnes remembered quite clearly that Neale had caught Barnabetta looking at the book of money while he had it in his possession at the winter quarters of the circus. At once the boy would connect the robbery of the Corner House with the circus girl's presence there.

And that would never do. For Agnes was positive that Barnabetta was guiltless of the final disappearance of the treasure trove.

But suppose Neale was convinced otherwise? With sorrow the Corner House girl had to admit that her boy friend could be "awful stubborn" if he so chose.

"And he might come right over here and say something cross to Barnabetta and to poor Mr. Scruggs, and then everybody'd be unhappy," Agnes told herself. "Barnabetta is repentant for all she did. It would be mean to accuse her of something she hadn't done at all."

So Agnes went rather soberly down the back yard paths to the end of the chicken run. She never contemplated for an instant going round by Willow Street and Willow Wythe to reach the cobbler's front door.

Only a high board fence separated the Corner House premises from the little back yard of Mr. Con Murphy. There was the corner where Neale got over, and Agnes was enough of a tomboy to know the most approved fashion of mounting the barrier.

But she hesitated a moment before she did this. Maybe Neale was not there. Maybe he was still so angry that he would not see her if she went into Con's little shop. She must cajole him.

Therefore she sent a tentative call over the back fence:

"Oh-ee! Oh-ee! Oh-ee!"

She waited half a minute and repeated it. But there was no answer.

"Oh, dear me!" thought Agnes. "Is he still huffy? Or isn't he home?"

She ventured a third call, but to no avail. Agnes, however, had a determined spirit. She felt that Neale might help them in the emergency which had arisen, and she proposed to get his help in some fashion.

So she started to climb the fence. Just as she did so—spang! A snowball burst right beside her head. She was showered with snow and, screeching, let go her hold and fell back into the Corner House yard.

"Oh! oh! oh! Who was that?" sputtered Agnes.

She glanced around under the bare-limbed trees and tried to peer into the shadows cast by the hen house and Billy Bumps' abode. Not a soul there, she was sure.

"Some boy going by on the street must have thrown it," Agnes thought. "But how could he see me away in here?"

She essayed to climb the fence again, and a second snowball—not quite as hard as the first—struck her right between the shoulder blades.

"Oh! you horrid thing!" exclaimed Agnes, turning to run toward the street fence. "I'd like to get my hands on you! I bet if Neale were here you wouldn't fling snowballs at a girl!"

"Don't blow too much about what Neale O'Neil would do!" cried a voice; and a figure appeared at the corner of the hen house.

"Oh! you horrid thing! Neale O'Neil! You flung those snowballs yourself!" gasped Agnes.

She was plucky and she started for him instantly, grabbing a good-sized handful of snow as she did so. Neale uttered a shout and turned to run; but he caught his heel in something and went over backward into the drift he himself had piled up at the hen house door when he had shoveled the path.

"I've got you—you scamp!" declared the Corner House girl, and fell upon him with the snowball and rubbed his face well with it. Neale actually squealed for mercy.

"Lemme up!"

"Got enough?"

"Yep!"

"Say 'enough,' then," ordered Agnes, cramming some more snow down the victim's neck.

"Can't—it tickles my tongue. Ouch! Look out! Your turn will come yet, miss."

"Do anything I say if I let you up?" demanded Agnes, who had half buried Neale by her own weight in the soft snow.

"Yep! Ouch! Don't! Play fair!"

"Then you'll come right into the house and talk to me and Ruthie about that awful money?" demanded Agnes, getting up.

Neale started to rise, and then sat back in the snow.

"What money?" he demanded.

"The money and bonds that were stuck into the old album."

"What about them?"

"Oh, Neale! Oh, Neale!" cried Agnes, on the verge of tears. "The money is gone."

"Huh?"

"It isn't in the book! We—we never looked till to-night, and—what do you think? Somebody got into the house and robbed us—of all that money! And it belonged to Mrs. Eland and her sister. Mr. Lemuel Aden hid it in our garret. Now! isn't that awful?"

For a minute Neale made no reply. Agnes thought he must be struck actually dumb by the horror and surprise which the announcement caused him. Then he made a funny noise and got up out of the snow. His face was in the shadow.

"What's the matter with you?" demanded Agnes. "Didn't you hear?"

"Yes—I heard," said Neale, in a peculiar tone. "What did you say about that stuff in the book?"

"Why, Neale! it is good. At least, the money is. Ruth went again to the bank and she is sure she had the right banknote examined this time. And, of course, if one was good the rest were!"

"Ye-es," said Neale, still speaking oddly. "But what about Mrs. Eland?"

"It belonged to her—all that money—and her sister. You see, Lemuel Aden stayed here at the old Corner House just before he died and he left this book here because he believed it would be safe. He said Uncle Peter was a fool, but honest. Horrid old thing!"

"Who—Uncle Peter?" asked Neale.

"No—Lemuel Aden. And then he went and died and never said anything about the money only in his diary, and Mrs. Eland showed it to Ruth in the diary, and Ruth knew what it meant, but she didn't tell Mrs. Eland. And now, Neale O'Neil, somebody's followed you down from that Tiverton place, knowing you had that book, and got into our house and taken all that money—"

"Gee, Aggie!" cried the boy, interrupting the stream of this monologue. "You'll lose your breath talking so much. Let's go in and see about this."

"Oh, Neale! Will you?"

"Yes. I was coming to call you out anyway," said the boy, gruffly. "You're a good kid, Aggie. But Ruth can be too fresh—"

"You don't know how worried she's been—how worried we've both been," Agnes said.

"That's all right. But I'm honest. I wouldn't have stolen that money."

"Of course not, Neale," cried Agnes, but secretly condemned because there had been a time when, for a few hours, she herself had almost doubted the honesty of the white-haired boy.

"But somebody must have seen it in your possession, and come down with you and stolen it."

"Huh! You think so?"

"How else can you explain it?" demanded the voluble Agnes, the pent up waters of her imagination overflowing now. "Of course it was very dangerous indeed for you to be carrying all that wealth around with you. Why, Neale! you might have been killed for it.

"The—the book was put in that old closet in the dining room chimney. And Aunt Sarah locked the door, not knowing there was anything of importance in the closet but her peppermints. And then we couldn't unlock it because the lock was fouled.

"And so, we don't know when the money was taken. But we broke the lock of the closet this afternoon and there it was—the book, I mean—empty!"

Neale was leading her toward the house. "Great Peter's pipe!" he gasped. "You can talk nineteen to the dozen and no mistake, Aggie. Hush, will you, till we get inside?"

Agnes was rather offended at this. She went up the porch steps ahead and opened the door into the hall. Ruth was just going into the sitting room.

"Oh, Ruthie! are you alone?" whispered Agnes.

"Goodness! how you startled me," said the older sister. "There's nobody in the sitting room. What do you want? Oh!"

"It's Neale," said Agnes, dragging the boy in. "And you've got to tell him how sorry you are for what you said!"

"Well—I like that!" exclaimed Ruth.

"You know you're sorry," pleaded the peacemaker. "Say so!"

"Well, I am! Come in, Neale O'Neil. Between us, you and I have made an awful mess of this thing. Mrs. Eland and Miss Pepperill have lost all their fortune."

"How's that?" asked the boy, easily.

"Didn't Agnes tell you that the money and bonds have been stolen?"

"Why—she said so," admitted Neale.

"Well!" exclaimed Ruth.

"Well!" exclaimed Agnes.

"I guess you are worried about not much of anything," said Neale O'Neil, lightly.

"What do you mean, you silly boy?" demanded Ruth, with rising asperity. "I tell you that money must have all been good money, whether the bonds were valuable or not."

It was then Neale's turn to say, "Well?"

"Neale O'Neil!" shouted Agnes, shaking him. "What are you trying to do—torment us to death? What do you know about this?"

"Why, I told you the old book was in my bag on the porch when I left here Saturday night," drawled the boy. "But do you suppose I would have flung it down there so carelessly if the money and bonds had been in it?"

CHAPTER XXV—AGNES IS PERFECTLY HAPPY

"Oh, Neale! Oh, Ruth! I'm going to faint!" murmured Agnes Kenway, and she sank into a chair and began to "stiffen out" in approved fainting fashion.

But when she saw the boy pick up a vase, grab the flowers out of it with ruthless hand, and start to douse her with the water it was supposed to contain, the Corner House girl "came to" very promptly.

"Don't do that!" she cried. "You'll spoil those roses. And if there was water in that vase it would ruin my dress. Goosey! Those are artificial flowers, anyway. That's all a boy knows!"

"Neale seems to know a great deal that we do not," Ruth said faintly, really more overcome than Agnes was by the bomb Neale had flung.

"Say! haven't you heard from Mr. Howbridge?" demanded the youth.

"Mr. Howbridge?" murmured Ruth. "No."

"Then he'll be home himself to-morrow, and thought it wasn't worth while to write."

"What do you mean, Neale O'Neil?" demanded Agnes.

"Did you see Mr. Howbridge?" asked Ruth.

"Sure!"

"But I thought you went to see your uncle, Mr. Sorber," said the oldest Corner House girl.

"So I did. Poor Uncle Bill! He was pretty well done up. But he's better now, as I told you. But that's why I took the old book with me."

"What is why?" demanded Agnes.

"Such 'langwitch'!" exclaimed Neale, with laughter. "I tell you I carried that album away with me because I wanted to show the stuff in it to Mr. Howbridge. I remembered he was up there in Tiverton, too."

"Oh, dear me! I had forgotten it!" cried Ruth.

"I remembered, but I forgot to tell you," said Agnes.

"I didn't think the stuff was any good. But I thought Mr. Howbridge ought to see it and judge for himself. So I took it to him. He was busy when I first called and I left the book with him. That was at his brother's house."

"Oh, Neale!" groaned Ruth. "Why didn't you write us about it?"

"Didn't think of it. I give you my word I did not believe that the bonds were worth anything; and I was confident the money was phony."

"Oh, dear!" said Agnes. "And it's all safe? Mr. Howbridge has all that great lot of money?"

"Yes. I saw him Saturday before I came down to Milton. He pretty nearly took me off my feet when he said that it was all good stuff, with lots of dividend money coming to the owner of the bonds, too. And he wanted to know all the particulars of your finding the album. Bless you! he doesn't know what to think about it. He is only sure that your Uncle Peter never owned the bonds or the cash."

"He didn't," sighed Agnes, "more's the pity. Oh, no, Ruthie. I am not sorry Mrs. Eland and Miss Pepperill are going to be rich. But we could have made good use of some of that money."

"Buying an automobile, for instance?" suggested Neale, chuckling.

"Be careful, young man," Agnes warned him. "If you carry a joke too far, you shall never be allowed to run the Corner House automobile when we do get it."

"I'll be good," said Neale, promptly. "For I have a sneaking sort of idea that maybe you will have one, Aggie, before long."

"Oh, Neale!"

"Fact. Somebody's going to get a bunch of money for finding that album. And you are the one who really made the find, Aggie Kenway."

"Now I know I shall faint!" gasped the next to the oldest Corner House girl.

"We wouldn't want money for giving Mrs. Eland what belongs to her," Ruth said quietly.

"Maybe not," said Neale, grimly. "But I guess Mr. Howbridge knows his business. He is your guardian. He will apply to the court for the proper reward for you, if it isn't forthcoming from the beneficiaries themselves."

"Goodness, Neale O'Neil! How you talk," said Agnes, in wonder. "You talk just like a lawyer yourself."

"Maybe I will be one some day," said the boy, diffidently. "But Mr. Howbridge talked a lot to me about the matter on Saturday. He said of course the real owners of the money and bonds must be hunted up. Perhaps he has some shrewd suspicion as to who they may be.

"But you girls have got rights in any treasure trove found in the old Corner House—"

"Gracious mercy me! I hope I shall find a lot more money and bonds," declared Agnes. "I'm going right up to the attic to-morrow and hunt some more."

But of course she did not. There were too many things happening on the morrow. Mr. Howbridge came from Tiverton and the girls found him at the Corner House when they came home from school.

He brought with him a statement showing how much money there was in that treasure trove found in the garret, and the value of the railroad bonds and the dividends due on them.

He was quite ready to believe Ruth's discovery regarding the true ownership of the treasure, too.

"I have heard Peter Stower often say that he wondered what Lemuel Aden did with his money. He stuck to it that Lem was a wealthy man, but the very worst kind of a miser.

"And that he should bring his wealth here and hide it in the old Corner House is not at all surprising. As a boy he played about here with your Uncle Peter. He knew the old garret as well as you children do, I warrant."

Later Mr. Howbridge went with Ruth to call on the matron of the Women's and Children's Hospital. Mrs. Eland produced the diaries and Mr. Howbridge read the notes referring to the old miser's "Beautiful Book."

It was decided by the Courts, at a later time, that the money and bonds all belonged to the two sisters, sole remaining heirs of Lemuel Aden. Mr. Howbridge acted for both parties in the transaction and nothing was said about any reward due the Corner House girls for making the odd find in the garret.

That is, there was little said about any reward just then. But Agnes went about with such a smiling face that everybody who knew her stopped to ask what it meant.

"Why, don't you know?" she said. "Just as soon as we can have it built, there will be a garage in our back yard. And Neale O'Neil is studying at the Main Street Garage every day after school, so he can run a car and take out a license like Joe Eldred. And—"

"But you haven't a car, Aggie Kenway!" cried Eva Larry, who was one of the most curious.

"Oh, no; not yet," drawled Agnes, with fine nonchalance. "But we're having one built for us. Mr. Howbridge himself ordered it for us. And it's going to be big enough to take out the whole Corner House family."

It was not that the other Corner House girls had no interest in this forthcoming pleasure car; but there were so many other things, to take up their attention.

Ruth was interested in getting Barnabetta and her father settled in two very nice rooms on Meadow Street for the winter. There they would remain until the circus season opened in the spring.

Barnabetta had secured a position for a few months that would support her and the clown; and Neale had written to his Uncle Bill Sorber and obtained a contract for the Scruggs' for the next season.

Miss Pepperill was back from the State Hospital and her sister and she were all ready to go across the Continent to remain a year at least. Milton people who knew her work, were sorry to see Mrs. Eland go. Her friends, however, were glad that never again would the little gray lady and her red-haired sister have to worry about ways and means.

As for the little girls, their interests were as varied as usual. But principally they were rejoicing that Sammy Pinkney was well on the road to health, Dr. Forsyth having brought him safely through the scarlet fever.

"And for a boy that's had quarantine and epidermis, too, all at the same time, it's quite wonderful," Dot said. "And—and there's a chance for him yet to grow up and be a pirate!"

THE END

9 781836 573029